INSANITY 4

HOOKAH

Cameron Jace

Other Books by Cameron Jace

The Grimm Diaries Prequels Series

The Grimm Diaries Prequels 1-6 (Free)

The Grimm Diaries Prequels 7-10

The Grimm Diaries Prequels 11-14

The Grimm Diaries Prequels 15-18

The Grimm Diaries Main Series

Snow White Sorrow (book 1)

Cinderella Dressed in Ashes (book 2)

Blood, Milk & Chocolate Part 1 (book3)

I Am Alive Series

I Am Alive (book 1)

Pentimento Series

Pentimento (book 1)

Books in the Insanity Series

Insanity

Figment

Circus

Hookah

How to read this book:

Begin at the beginning
and go until you come to the end;
then stop.

In the memory of Lewis Carroll.
We love you for the madman you were.

Prologue Part One

The man in the priest's outfit landed in the middle of Oxford University in an automobile strapped up in helium balloons.

Students craned their necks up, recognizing the aero-engined car, a British masterpiece powered by aircraft engines that some thought could fly back in the 1920's.

But never had they seen it hinged on balloons like today.

Against normal laws of physics, the car descended to the ground, and people stared at it as if it was an alien spaceship.

After landing, the man in the priest's outfit stepped out of the automobile, flashing a broad smile at the world. His hair was swept by a swirling breeze, and his lanky stature was considerably attractive. He looked familiar to the children attending this celebration. His image had been carved in the back of their heads since they first started reading.

There was no mistaking it. The man looked like an uncanny modern day incarnation of Lewis Carroll.

Not just that. The man had arrived with what every child in the world had been craving for a while—and it wasn't candy.

"Where are the hookahs?" a child said. "You said you'd bring the Hookah of Hearts!"

Amidst the flashing cameras and the nosey reporters, the man flapped his hands sideways like a living scarecrow from the Wizard of Oz. He was about to show them his latest trick.

Behind him, the sky drizzled, not rain but gift-wrapped packages.

"It's raining hookahs, hallelujah," The man said in a soft voice.

The hookahs inside the packages, like his car, dangled from hundreds of brightly colored helium balloons.

The children hoorayed and ran toward them, tiptoeing, reaching, and competing for one of their own.

More flashes. TV Cameras. People with microphones broadcasting the frabjous event.

The Hookah of Hearts had been in the market for more than a year. Manufactured by Dodo, a mysterious toy company obsessed with everything Alice in Wonderland—the caterpillar and his hookah in particular.

The children began collecting their presents, ripping apart the wrappers and pulling out their hookahs.

They began smoking them.

Everyone applauded.

Of course they weren't puffing real smoke like adults. Those were mini hookahs. The children sucked on some unique scent -- the flavor of Tiger Lilies -- which was harmless, and puffed out bubbles instead of smoke.

Pink bubbles. Blue bubbles. Green bubbles.

Occasionally there was this one bubble that wrote words like *who are you?* in the air.

The crowd applauded again. Enthusiastic. Feeling fantastic. Some of them even felt... *frantastic.*

More and more flashes.

The broadcasting cameras rotated back toward the Lewis Carroll look-a-like priest.

He looked incredibly uncomfortable with the cameras, shielding his eyes with his hand. But the cameramen didn't care. This was even better than paparazzi's photos.

The reporters wondered how much such an extensive marketing campaign cost the Dodo Corporation.

"Come on. The car and flying hookahs must have cost a fortune. They can't be real, or...?"

The man wore his smile thinner, and said nothing. He looked like he had a toothache, his jaw twitching a little.

Another reporter asked him if it was true that over six million hookahs had been sold worldwide.

Still irritated by the flashes, he continued saying nothing.

However, he responded to the children who had questions about certain functions in the hookahs.

"May I compliment your outfit and make up, sir." A young female reporter stuck her microphone—and nose—out of the squeezing crowd. "I mean, you really look like the legendary Lewis Carroll. How is that even possible?"

This time, the priest looked amused. It was the question he'd been waiting for. "Y-y-young la-lady," he stuttered like Lewis Carroll did in real life. "What makes you think I'm not him?"

Prologue Part Two

Some of TV crew rolled their eyes at the man's reply. Others laughed at the unmatched confidence and acting.

But something about him was so original. The way he said the words.

An uncomfortable silence swept over the university. A silence that spread to every TV set in every home all over the world.

Who was this man, really?

"M-my name is Lewis Ca-car-roll." The man bowed in front of the camera. "A-and I've come to bestow my b-b-beautiful madness u-u-upon this world."

The silence stretched for a few more seconds.

It was like staring at a clown. No one was really sure what to expect. Should they have panicked and ran away, or just laughed and said, 'Haha, of course you are!'

Too many so-called Wonderland Monsters had been to London lately: the creepy Cheshire, the Muffin Man, and the Mad Hatter with his rabbit bomb last week. It had become impossible to dismiss someone claiming he was one of them.

A few kids managed to break the silence, coughing bubbles and flowers from sucking on the hookahs.

Those bubbles weren't pink. They weren't blue. They weren't green.

"Why are the children coughing... red bubbles?" the young reporter asked.

"Silly me. I forgot," the priest said, stepping back into his flying car and pulling a lever that pumped air into more balloons. "Our Hookah of Hearts, which has already sold more than six million pieces all over the world, well, it's not just a hookah." The balloons began to take off again. "This hookah holds a deadly disease like nothing you've ever seen."

Faces began to redden, confused by the man's continued speech of madness.

Was he joking? Why would the Dodo Corporation send a loon like him to represent them?

"And I repeat"—his smile broadened, too wide to be benevolent—"a deadly virus like nothing you've seen before. It should start working in a few hours. Within three days"—the automobile hovered above the ground—"this world as you know it will end."

What once was silence escalated to ascending grunts of panic. More children kept coughing. Parents worried, watching him escape into the sky. More people in the world couldn't believe what they were watching on the news.

"Who are you?" a reporter screamed at the floating priest.

"I told you. My name is Lewis Carroll," he said from high above, looking like someone sweet and colorful in the middle of a never-ending nightmare. "And I am a Wonderland Monster."

Chapter 1

St Peter's Basilica, the Vatican

I am waiting in line to enter the confession room so I can talk to Fabiola.

Tens of men and women entered the booth before me, most of them slouched by the weight of whatever truth, or sins, they were about to confess.

But knowing Fabiola—from the few times we've met—I'm aware of her positive influence on people.

Until it's my turn, I fiddle with the key Lewis Carroll gave me three weeks ago when I first met him through the Tom Tower.

I pulled it out of my cell's wall this morning, fearing it wasn't safe in there anymore. Not after I stupidly lost another key to the Mad Hatter last week. I messed up. Who knows what this Hatter would do with it.

But this golden key in my hand—Lewis instructed me not to lose it under any circumstances. I plan not to disappoint him.

I'm looking forward to knowing why it's so important, along with the date scribbled on the walls of my cell in the asylum: January the 14th.

I wonder what happened on that day. If I could only remember why I wrote it on the wall—and if it was me who did it.

An old lady pats me on my shoulder, informing me that it's my turn.

I stand up, take a deep breath and enter the booth, waiting for Fabiola to slide open the window in between.

In the dark and silence of the booth, I'm reminded of Jack. Silly Jack who would never give up on me.

Silly Jack who may be only a figment of my imagination. A figment so nice I can't risk finding out he's not real.

"Are you here for a confession, Alice?" Fabiola asks behind the closed window. I wonder if the White Queen can see through walls.

"No," I say. "How can I confess what I don't remember?"

"Trust me." I hear her fingernails on the wooden frame. "It's a lot easier than trying to confess what you actually remember."

I lower my gaze and fiddle with the key, assuming Fabiola's heard humanity's darkest secrets between these walls.

"The Pillar lent you his plane to come and see me?" she says.

"Yes. But he doesn't know what I want to see you about."

"And what do you want to see me about?"

"Did you hear about me entering a delirious version of Wonderland through the Garden of Cosmic Speculation last week?"

"I did," Fabiola says. "I too had a vision that I met you inside and showed you the Impossible Six."

"Lewis, you, the March Hare, Jack, me, and a little girl."

"If you're here to ask me about the little girl, I have no answer for you... at least not now."

"I admit I am curious, but it's not what I'm here for."

"Why are you here then, Alice?" Fabiola sounds impatient. I get the feeling she is afraid that talking to me for longer periods will force her to confess too much to me.

The irony.

"I think what I saw was some kind of epiphany, a sign for me to do something," I say. "I want to gather the Impossible Six and create an opposing force against Black Chess."

Fabiola slides open the window.

Chapter 2

"**Y**ou want to stand up to the Queen of Hearts and Black Chess?" Fabiola's eyes show concern.

"I don't want to wait for the monster of the week anymore," I say. "I know about the Circus. How it all started. Black Chess has to be stopped."

"You know nothing at all, believe me. But it's admirable that, although you're not sure if you're the Real Alice, you want to play the hero's part."

"I don't care if I'm her or not. All I know is that I can stop bad things from happening in this world."

"Did you think about the price you will have to pay?"

"Other than living in a mad world where I can't tell what's real from what's not? Yes, I know I want to do this."

"It's not that easy. Black Chess is darkness itself. Stare into it too long and it will stain you with a black veil of unforgettable pain."

I shrug, tightening my grip on the key. "I believe the world can be a better place, only if the truth, in this case Black Chess, is exposed and defeated."

"The truth," Fabiola considers. "I'm not sure we all want to know about it. What do you have in mind?"

"Like I said, gather the good guys. Jack is with me in the asylum.

I will find a way to get the March Hare out of the Hole. I'm not sure where Lewis stands in all of this. I mean, is he alive or dead? But I'm not worried about him, not as much as the little girl."

"The time hasn't come to talk about her yet," Fabiola says. "So I'd postpone looking for her, same goes for Lewis. He has a war of his own, so he'll show up when it's his time."

My eyes meet hers. "And you?"

"What about me?"

"Are you in? If so, my impression is that you'd be the leader."

"Normally I would be. But I am not wearing my white outfit to entice wars. I wear it to wipe off the old days of Wonderland, when I had blood all over my hands."

I am oblivious to whatever she is talking about.

"My time and strength are devoted to the people who seek peace in this world," she follows. "I may give advice, be resourceful, but I'm not going to be part of the Wonderland War when it begins. My real war is to avoid war."

I am disappointed. I was hoping she'd help, instead of me having to deal with the Pillar's devious ways—he isn't one of the good guys. I am not sure whose side he is on.

"At least bless us with a name instead of the Impossible Six." I let out an uncomfortable chuckle.

"It's already been picked," she says. "The Inklings."

"Already been picked?"

"There was a prophecy in Wonderland: that Alice will return and put an end to Black Chess. Of course, we're not going to argue whether you're her or not again."

"A prophecy." I wonder if that's why the Pillar found me. "Inklings?"

"It's named after a meeting place. A bar known as the Bird, previously known as the Eagle and Child. It's near Oxford University. It's a special place. Great people who stood in the face of evil before you attended it regularly."

"Anyone I know?"

"Of course." She finally smiles. "J. R. R. Tolkien and C. S. Lewis, who wrote the Lord of the Rings and the Chronicles of Narnia."

I tilt my head.

Fabiola senses my confusion. "The Inklings was the name of an elite writers group who met at the bar. Lewis Carroll spent most of his time there, almost a century before Tolkien and C. S. Lewis came, when it wasn't a bar yet. It's said they found some of his diaries in there. It was why they attended regularly in the first place."

"Pardon me, but the connection escapes me, Fabiola. Those writers knew about...?"

"The Wonderland Wars," Fabiola says. "What did you think those epic fantasies, the Lord of the Rings and Narnia, were about?"

No words come out of my mouth. I'm starting to realize how Wonderland is connected to everything.

"They were meant to inspire generations and educate them about the idea of good and evil in this world." Fabiola stops to make sure I am following. "They were discreetly using literature to prepare generations for the Wonderland Wars."

Chapter 3

The Eagle and Bird Bar, Oxford

The chauffeur watched the Pillar knock his cane on the floor for the hundredth time.

His employer had been sitting alone in this old bar for some time, staring at a golden key in his hand. Rarely had the chauffeur seen the Pillar so gloomy, not the flamboyant and out-of-this-world man he usually was.

The Pillar had just bought this old bar. For over half a million pounds.

The chauffeur wondered if he'd spent that money to tap a cane and stare at a key. Why this bar? There were dozens of old historical bars in Oxford, many of them truly profitable.

The chauffeur wondered if the Pillar had heard of the new Wonderland Monster calling himself Lewis Carroll yet.

Would he be just sitting here if he had?

The Pillar didn't look like he wanted to talk to anyone.

"So should I employ someone to run this place?" the chauffeur hissed.

"No need," the Pillar answered, eyes still on the key. "Alice will run the place herself soon. I'm anxious to see if she'd serve good tea like the Hatter back in Wonderland."

"Alice?"

"Well, let's say she's about to finally pick up her team and oppose Black Chess." The Pillar tucked the key next to his watch inside his breast pocket. He tapped his pocket gently with his white-gloved hand. "The first real step into the War."

"So it's really happening?"

"Wars are inevitable, my lousy driver." The Pillar stood up and elegantly flipped his cane. "Victories aren't."

"Wars like these?" The chauffeur turned on the TV. The six o'clock news was covering the incident with the creepy Lewis Carroll look-a-like claiming he'd spread an incurable plague to the world.

"That's just the tip of the iceberg," the Pillar said. "I hope you didn't smoke any of those toy hookahs yourself."

"Not at all, Professor. I'm not into puffing bubbles," the chauffeur prided himself. "But if I may ask: is the plague real?"

"Looks too real, in fact."

The chauffeur wasn't sure what that meant.

"Get my plane ready," the Pillar said, slowly easing into a better mood.

"That plane is in the Vatican. You just let Alice use it this morning."

"Not that plane." The Pillar knocked his cane against the floor.

The chauffeur swallowed hard. "You mean the War Plane?"

The Pillar nodded, momentarily closing his eyes. "In fact, I want all my planes ready and handy. The choppers, too. Don't forget the guns."

They hadn't used the planes since the Pillar went on a rampage, killing twelve people some time ago. "Where are we going, Professor?"

"We're going to pay a visit to darkness itself," the Pillar said, diverting his focus on the broadcasting news. "Welcome home Lewis Carroll. It's been some time."

Chapter 4

The Eagle and Bird Bar, Oxford
An hour after the Pillar left

I received the Pillar's call a few hours ago while I was still in the Vatican. He'd given me the address to the Inklings bar with the location of its key in a Tiger Lily pot beside the door.

I picked up the key and entered the place. On the table, there was a contract in my name. The Pillar bought me the headquarters of my Inklings gathering place.

Unfortunately, I didn't have much time to look at the historical signatures of the likes of Tolkien and C.S. Lewis on the walls. I was stopped, and shocked, by the news about the Lewis Carroll man on TV

Now I am standing, staring at the TV in awkward awe.

Is this for real?

The man in the news looks just like the Lewis Carroll I saw through the Tom Tower and Einstein's Blackboard.

Lewis Carroll is a Wonderland Monster?

"This can't be," I say to emptiness.

"I thought so, too." The Pillar's chauffeur appears out of nowhere. "But whoever he is, you need to look at this."

He points at the BBC's world coverage of what looks like people coughing red bubbles all over the world.

The BBC says that doctors haven't found a medical explanation for it. Nothing in the hookahs shows a hostile infection of any sort. Still, it's spreading fast, and they're worried it'll lead to a disaster in a few hours.

"The Pillar assured me this is the beginning of an unimaginable plague," the chauffeur says.

"People coughing red bubbles. What kind of plague is that?"

"The Pillar said you'd say that, so he recorded this little video for you." He shows me a YouTube video on his phone.

"Think about it, Alice. Have you ever seen anyone cough bubbles, let alone red? Do as my chauffeur tells you." The Pillar drags from his hookah. "Ah, and don't forget to sign the contract. Congrats, you own a bar now. At least you have a job, in case you lose your career as a magnificent lunatic patient in the asylum."

The video ends.

I look at the contract, not sure if I should accept a half a million pound gift. I tell myself Fabiola would accept it; the Inklings is part of the prophecy.

I sign both the Pillar's and my copy, not reading through.

As I hand it back to the chauffeur, I glimpse a condition in the contract written at the bottom of the page:

The two parties who share the Inklings Bar are bound by the agreement in this contract for an unknown time. The contract is automatically cancelled once Alice saves the world from every last Wonderland Monster.

"Would you kindly seal the envelope?" the chauffeur suggests. "The Pillar demanded you seal his copy yourself so I don't peek into it."

"Trust issues?" I roll my eyes, both at the request and the lines in the contract, then lick the envelope to seal it.

But it's a short roll of eyes, and a shorter lick, only half way through. I find myself swirling down to the floor like a dying flower.

The envelope's tip contains some kind of sedative. The Pillar's drugged me again.

Chapter 5

Pillar's Plane,
Somewhere next to a mushroom cloud

I wake up to the suffocating and blurry waves of hookah smoke.

Coughing, I part the drapes of smoking curtains and feel my way through this delirium. At the end of the maze, I come to find the Pillar sitting on his favorite couch, dragging and puffing while fiddling with his hookah's hose.

"I thought I'd bring the couch with me," he says. "What's a man without his favorite couch?"

Instead of screaming and pulling hair, I look around and figure out where I am. I may have been a fool for licking the envelope, but I can still tell I'm inside a plane.

An air bump shakes the flight momentarily. I grab for the nearest seat but end up slumping next to the Pillar on the couch.

He doesn't lose balance. "Never understood what an air bump is," he says. "I mean, could we have bumped into a giant mushroom cloud up here?"

"Not funny," I adjust myself on the couch, and now the flight is normal again.

"Want to see what's really not funny?" He clicks on the TV. "We have a new Wonderland Monster."

I am watching the same news I saw in the Inklings, only things are getting worse now. People don't just cough red bubbles. They're starting to get edgy after it, looking rather mean, like they're about to hurt one another.

"Who is this Wonderland Monster, really?" I ask. "The Cheshire?"

"The Cheshire can't possess any of the main Wonderlanders, in case you didn't notice." The Pillar sets the hookah aside and waves off some smoke. "But you're also right."

"Meaning?"

"The man is Lewis Carroll."

"That can't be. Lewis isn't a monster. He is the one who locked the monsters in Wonderland."

"I guess he forgot to lock himself in, too. Or, how about he just made you believe he isn't a monster in the Tom Tower?" The Pillar's face is unreadable. Is he telling the truth? "The man was nuts. Migraines and split personality. He was schizophrenic. Left handed and unable to hear with his right ear. It all happened particularly after the events of the Circus. He lost his grip on reality when he relied on drugs to ease his mind from the trauma."

"I don't believe a word you're saying."

"I didn't believe I'd ever grow up and become old when I was a kid, either," he says." I mean, why would God do this to me? I was having a great time being small and unnoticed, doing whatever I wanted."

Like usual, I pass on commenting. "So Lewis was really using drugs?"

"Drugs were still legal until the middle of the 19th century." He pulls out an 80's cassette player and squeezes a tape inside.

"Really?" I can't understand how. Things like this, and the Circus, make me look at humanity from a new and different perspective. How could drugs have been legal only a century and a half ago?

"In the eyes of society, and himself, Lewis wasn't doing anything wrong at the time." He pushes the sticky button. Melodies of White

Rabbit by Jefferson Airplane blast out of the worn-out cassette player. The Pillar begins his Caucus Race dance. "A lot of writers, including Charles Dickens, took those legal drugs at the time. Makes you wonder if he could have produced his masterpieces without them." He winks. "But all geniuses have a vice, don't they?" He points at his hookah. "Besides, really, read that Alice in Wonderland book again. It's full of hallucinations and madness. Maybe the dude was a little tipsy when wrote it."

I'm not fond of him talking about Lewis like that, but I need to hear more first.

"Lewis had issues, so what?" The Pillar shakes his shoulders. "We just don't like to talk about them, so we continue living in our la-la world." He stretches his arms sideways and imitates a bird's wings while half-circling in place. "My moves are getting better."

"I want to know all you know about Lewis." I feel offended, suddenly realizing how much I love Lewis.

"The world is falling apart, Alice." He points at the TV. "Look at those angry faces walking around. Lewis Carroll told the press it would take three days to end the world, so I assume the symptoms will worsen at rocket speed." He pulls out an oversized clock from behind his bag and tucks it in my lap. "The clock is ticking. We don't have time. We need to find a cure for the plague. Listen. Tick. Tock."

I put the clock away. It's not even working. "So Lewis Carroll was behind manufacturing the Hookahs of Hearts all over the world, hiding behind that Dodo Company? I thought it was Black Chess."

"It's not," the Pillar says. "Which is why it's intriguingly puzzling." The Pillar fetches something else from behind the couch. "But we're minutes...I mean seconds away from finding out." He pulls out two parachutes and throws one at me, as if I'm expected to be an expert with it. "I hope you know how to use a parachute because this plane is going to explode..."

"What?"

"Dress up, and prepare to fly, Alice. It's not that different from falling into a rabbit hole." He straps on his parachute and checks his pocket watch. "All we have is about...let's say thirty seconds before this plane explodes?"

Chapter 6

"**W**hy will the plane explode?"

The Pillar doesn't answer me, tightening the straps of his parachute and putting on his goggles. "Do I look good?"

Even if I was planning to keep cool, I can't. Kneeling down, I pick up the parachute and try to put it on. I have never worn one before.

"Excellent." He is already strapped into his, looking ready. The White Rabbit song in the background is driving me crazy.

I am not sure I am doing this right. I keep strapping whatever I find around me. Is this supposed to be like this, or is it supposed to be upside down?

"Here." He throws my umbrella toward me. I hardly catch it as I am still strapping my parachute. "You'll need this fantabulous weapon of yours down there."

"Where are we going?" The words sputter out of my lips. I'm almost done with strapping. Who in their right mind ties themselves up in a parachute not knowing how to land it?

"You," the Pillar addresses his chauffeur flying the plane. "You're good with dying for the cause, right?"

The back of my head hurts when I hear this. The chauffeur is going to stay in the plane when it explodes?

"The men down below have to think we have no one to pick us up, you understand?" the Pillar tells his chauffeur.

True, I understand nothing, but I've finally managed to put my parachute on.

"Ten seconds." The Pillar raises his voice as the plane's rear door opens, a swirl of wind kickboxing against my body. "So here is the thing," he shouts. "Lewis Carroll's plague is like nothing I've ever seen. I had a few science labs check it. They didn't find anything wrong with the hookahs. My guess is that it's a hallucinogenic. Some substance that drives you mad when you smell it."

I am not sure if I can hear the rest. It's not that the air plastering my face but that my heart is racing when I see how far below the earth is.

"Five seconds," the Pillar continues. "The only ones I know who have the power to create this are ex-Wondelranders who live among us. Those Wonderlanders are the lowest scum of the world. They'd kill you only to take a selfie of your blood on their faces and send it to your mom so they could laugh at the horrified expression on her face. Understand?"

"Shouldn't we jump already?" I shout, hardly interested in what he says.

"Trust me, jumping Is the least of your worries. Those men below could eat us for dessert. So you have to think about it. If you can't do it, you can simply stay here and explode with my chauffeur."

"Fabulous choices." I am so ready to jump, although I don't know how. What the heck is wrong with me? "If you keep babbling, I'm jumping before you."

The Pillar smiles. "Wait, don't jump without this." He hands over a pair of cool black goggles. "Here is a tip." He struggles shouting against the wind. "Always look cool on your way down the rabbit hole. Never do it Elvis style."

"You mean because he was found dead with his head in the toilet?"

"Nah." The Pillar adjusts his goggles. "Because he died with his ass out at the world."

Chapter 7

Midair

Have you ever jumped out of a plane in a parachute, down to meet up with people who'd take selfies of your blood on their faces for breakfast?

I am doing it right now. And guess what, it's nighttime, so not only am I free-falling, but I am also doing it in the dark. That's what I call a bonus.

Throwing away the Pillar's goggles, I hear the plane explode in midair above me.

Oh my god, this is for real!

"I've always wanted to blow up my employees," the Pillar shouts all the way down. I am not sure how I can hear him. "But you'll be fine. Just pull the red lever when I tell you to."

In spite of all the madness, I feel unexpectedly fine up here in the air. Fine is an understatement. I feel euphoric. I want to feel like this every day. It's ridiculous how much I am enjoying this, although I may get face-palmed by the earth in a few seconds.

Mary Ann, also known as Alice Wonder, 19 years old, dead and gone. I imagine the scripture on my grave says. *But who cares? She was mad anyways.*

Suddenly I realize that the madness hasn't started yet. Not at all.

Down below, I can see something glittering. The vast land where we're landing is nothing but an endless field of ridiculously over-sized mushrooms.

Big mushrooms growing everywhere, whitening up the black of the night.

"Now!" the Pillar yells. "Pull the lever."

It's not easy to see it, so I pull whatever lever my hands come across. What? You think I might push the lever that expedites the fall?

I feel a sudden impact in my shoulders. So powerful I think I am close to dislocating both of them.

Off with their shoulders!

But it's only moments before it gets even better—or worse. The Pillar and I are floating in the air as we slowly begin our descent.

I try not to laugh myself silly as he pulls out a fishing pole and pretends to be fishing. "A man has to kill the boredom while landing. I can't tell you how excited I am now."

"For what exactly?" I say.

"Columbia, of course!"

Chapter 8

Buckingham Palace, London

The Queen of England—discreetly known as the Queen of Hearts—spat on the flowers in her garden.

She jumped in place, angry with the terribly red flowers. Unfortunately, no matter how high she jumped, she was still shorter than the average queen anywhere in the world.

But she was used to that. Ever since Wonderland her height had been her worst nightmare. She remembered having built a tall throne for herself she had to climb up with a ladder, so she could rule and be feared, only to realize how small she looked atop it.

Her own people had made fun of her that day.

However, the Queen always had a solution to shut them up—forever. She'd cut several thousand heads off, silencing the rest of the Wonderlanders.

Off with their heads!

That phrase never ceased to amaze her. It had the power to instantly put things in their place.

Thanks to King Henry VIII, the Queen thought, the Tudor madman whom she had learned the trick from. King Henry had chopped off more heads than anyone else in history—most of them were his wives'.

Most people didn't know he was a Wonderlander, and that his ghost still roamed the darker corridors of Oxford University.

Lewis Carroll had based the phrase on the king. But that was another Wonderland memory for another time.

Right now, the Queen's problem was with her flowers.

"Why are my flowers red?" she yelled in a loudspeaker she could barely grip with her small fatty hands.

"I thought you liked your flowers red, My Queen," Margaret Kent, the Duchess, replied.

"I like my flowers white!"

Margaret looked confused. Everyone who'd ever read Alice in Wonderland knew the Queen liked to paint her flowers red as she chopped off some heads. "But you've always liked them red," she argued. "Ever since Wonderland you prompted us to paint them red."

"See?" the Queen sighed. "That's the problem with you stupid people. What's your IQ, Margaret? Five and a half marshmallows? Do you even have a brain behind your surgically-enhanced face? Why didn't you opt for a better brain instead of a prettier face to address the nation?"

Most guards in the room wanted to laugh, the Queen knew. But none of them would risk their heads being cut off. It was a scientific fact: you couldn't live without a head unless you were the headless horseman from Sleepy Hollow.

"I'm sorry," Margaret said. "I thought you like to paint all roses red, so I found a genetically-enhanced species that grows only red flowers. It was designed by the March Hare, and I filled the castle with it."

Of course Margaret wasn't sorry, the Queen knew again. This duchess was a vicious woman who only bent over for her queen. There was a reason for that—and it wasn't respect.

"And what am I going to order my guards to paint red now?" The Queen stepped up on a chair and roared in the loudspeaker. "Here is the logic of it. I paint white roses red because they are white. The purpose is to suppress their nature and force them to turn into the color I want. It's a psychological thing. A Queen's thing. A message for the masses. Whatever your color is, I will color you my way. Do you get it?"

Margaret nodded.

"So when the flowers are red, I am losing my argument," the Queen followed. "Now I have no choice but to force everyone to only sell white flowers in England."

"Only white?"

"Yes, from this day on, England only sells white flowers." She jabbed a finger in the air. "What a brilliant idea." She jumped off her chair and adjusted her stiff troll-like hair. "Not only that. I want the Parliament to have a meeting and issue a law that prohibits the use of *white* flowers."

"But that's contradictory"

"And beautiful!" The Queen grinned. "Let's mess with those obnoxious human citizens. Let's see what they can do about it."

"As you wish, My Queen." Margaret chewed on the words. "On the side, I wanted you to take a look at another Wonderland Monster who showed up today, if you don't mind."

"I have no time for your silly requests, Margaret," the Queen dismissed her. "I'm more interested in the results of last week's Event. Please tell me my employees are wreaking havoc and madness all over the world. Please. Please. Please tell me they are driving the world mad."

Chapter 9

Columbia

I land and bounce on a fluffy large mushroom—did I really say that? Well, it's the truth. Way crazier than the Alice in the books.

It's a huge mushroom, coated with what would make a perfect mattress. Yet it's both bumpy and has a jelly feel to it on a few spots. I curl my body, tangled in my parachute, and roll on until I fall off the edge, right into the mud.

Splash!

Somewhere behind me, the Pillar laughs.

It irks me. I am not going to play clumsy in here. Not in Columbia.

Curling out of the tangled parachute is not an easy task. When I am done, I realize the parachute is painted to look like a huge mushroom from above. I twitch, glancing at the Pillar, who's standing up straight, his suit perfectly clean, and lighting up a cigar.

"I had the parachutes painted for camouflage purposes." His eyes look beady, enjoying his smoke. "You see, this place where we're standing now is off the charts. You can't find it on a map. Of course, you know where Columbia is, but you can never spot where Mushroomland is exactly."

"Mushroomland?" I trudge heavily in the mud.

"Indeed. This is where all the profitable drugs, hallucinogens, and a few other mischievous plants are grown."

"Those mushrooms are drugs?"

"Just like in the Alice in Wonderland books." Oh, he is enjoying his smoke. "Why did you think one side of the mushroom made you grow taller and the other made you smaller, or whatever that nonsense was?"

"I was being drugged, in a children's book?"

"Well, that's debatable." He marches on through the huge mushrooms.

"What's debatable?" I pick up my umbrella and follow him into the semi-darkness.

"That Alice in Wonderland is a children's book—but I don't have time for such debates." He crouches, investigating the premises. I crouch, too. "You see, Alice. Mushroomland is like Neverland. You're supposed to think it's unreal while it is not. No satellite up in the sky can track it. No one is supposed to talk about it. If you die in here, you're not only going to die alone, badly, but the authorities all around the world will ditch any evidence of your existence."

"Why all that?" I am whispering. I sense we're not alone. Danger is on its way. I still need to know why the Pillar thinks this place is where we can get a cure for the plague. Wasn't facing the Wonderland Monster in London a better strategy?

"Mushroomland grows ninety percent of the hallucinogens in the world," the Pillar says. "You may think these are a bunch of Columbian vagabonds controlling the drug business, but in reality they are funded by..."

"Black Chess," I cut in, thinking I am smart.

"Nah, wrong," he says. "But I'll get to that in a minute." We walk ahead cautiously. The moon is the only light I can see next to the orange hue from the Pillar's cigar. "Those mushrooms aren't just drugs. They have a substance that controls people's minds in the world. Some of them are in your every day food you buy from the market. Fizzy drinks, chocolates, and even vegetables. Why do you think they never stop marketing this stuff? Some of it is even sprinkled in the air."

"What? Why?"

"To numb you." He bites on his cigar. "So you feel cool about paying your taxes, tolerating the violence and madness in the world. Hell, some of these are electromagnetic mushrooms that affect your thinking on election days."

"You're joking, right?"

"Left." He winks.

I didn't expect that nonsensical answer. I was expecting a 'wrong' or 'right.' But this is the Pillar I am talking to.

"I'm not joking. You asked me who is funding Mushroomland? I'd say most of the world's high caliber governments."

"So what are we looking for in here? Are we looking to meet someone who can help us find the cure?"

The Pillar nods, now staring through some night-vision binoculars.

"Who exactly are we looking for?"

"The most ruthless, mind-bent man in the world."

"Does he have a name?"

"Of course he has a name." The Pillar stands up abruptly and walks on.

When I follow him, I realize we have company.

Men approaching us. Men with machine guns. This doesn't look good at all. I understand now what the Pillar meant when he said they'd take selfies of your blood on their faces, and I don't think we're getting out of here alive. At least, not both of us.

"Don't say a word," he hisses from the corner of his mouth. "And raise your hands. Eyes to the ground."

I do, feeling the weight of the approaching men, listening to the Pillar talk.

"We've come here in peace," he says. "In the name of all mushroom and hookahs and all trippy things."

"What are you looking for in here?" I hear a man with an accent and a gruff voice inquire.

"I'm looking for a man. A very important man," the Pillar says, and now I'm about to know the name of the most ruthless drug trafficker in the world. "The Executioner!"

Chapter 10

Mushroomland, Columbia

The Columbian men start laughing.

Although I can't make out their faces in the dark, their laughs send out waves that rattle the mushrooms all around me.

I must be really losing my mind. I mean really, like the acute pain of a heartache when you know for sure that it's over.

What the heck am I saying?

"Who do you think you are to meet with the Executioner?"

"I have two reasons to believe he wants to see me." The Pillar's words come out muffled with that cigar in his mouth. "Besides, I know about the Trail of Mushrooms."

The men's laughter grows louder. "You think you can pass the Trail of Mushrooms?"

"I'd like to try," the Pillar says. "I burned my plane with my pilot in it, after all. I have no means of going back to where I came from, so I have no choice but try or die."

"What's the Trail of Mushrooms?" I hiss in his ear.

"It's a pilgrimage. A road that has to be passed among the mushrooms," the Pillar whispers, not looking back at me. "We have to take it if we want to meet with the Executioner."

"And why is he called the Executioner?"

"He's a Wonderlander who used to work for the Queen. Remember that scene in the Alice books when the queen orders him to cut off the Cheshire's head and he argues that you can't cut a head that's disappearing?"

"Oh, yes, although most people would forget about him," I say. "But he didn't look scary to me."

"Like most of the other monsters, he turned into a beast after the Circus, except that he works on his own, and doesn't like any of the Wonderlanders much. Now shut up and let me speak with those madmen."

"Here is something for you," one of the men says. "We're sending you a man who's been trying to pass the Mushroom Trail."

"I thought most men die from the dangers of the trail. Either die or make it to the Executioner."

The men laugh again. "Well, this one ate a lot of mushrooms and lost it, so we keep him for entertainment purposes."

We stare at a half-naked and skinny man barely straightening his back as he walks toward us. He is old, skinny, and disoriented.

"Why is he so unstable?" The Pillar asks.

"He thinks he is walking the rope." A man muses from afar.

We wait for the man to arrive.

"Nice job," the Pillar plays along. "I've never seen a man walk a rope like that."

"I'm not walking the rope," the scruffy man retorts. "I'm being careful while walking. Can't you see I'm a bottle of milk?"

I am going to burst out laughing.

The Pillar pushes the man to the ground. "I guess I spilled the milk now." He raises his head at the men afar. "Listen, I have no time for games. Let me walk the trail to meet the Executioner. I will take my chances."

Silence hovers all over Mushroomland, except for the faint rattling of grass.

One of the men approaches us.

Slowly, he shows up. Scarred, wasted, a muscular giant with a machine gun.

Normally, I would be worried, but I don't know what's gotten into me. I want to laugh even more now.

The man flashes his gun toward the Pillar. "I'll let you pass," he says in a foreign accent. "If you tell me the password."

"There is no password." The Pillar steps up to him.

"Of course there is." The man nudges the muzzle of his machine gun against the Pillar's chest. "Can you do division?"

"As in mathematics?"

"Yes, but not the stupid real life mathematics. The Lewis Carroll mathematics."

This is when the need to laugh ends. How do these men at the other side of the world know about Lewis Carroll? Not just that. The man is about to tell us a Carroll puzzle to solve?

"Only a few people are allowed to see the Executioner. They all are capable of answering this question," the man says.

"I'm listening." The Pillar and I await the puzzle.

"In mathematical Wonderland terms, what do you get when you divide a loaf by a knife?"

Chapter 11

Another Lewis Carroll puzzle. Ugh.

That's all that comes to mind, and I have no idea why I am thinking this. Staring at the man with the machine gun I should act more mature and responsible, but I still have this strange feeling; I just want to burst out laughing like him.

"I don't quite remember this," the Pillar says. Is that possible, a puzzle he doesn't know of?

"It's simple mathematics," the man says. "Wonderlastic Mathematics, if I may say so."

"Look," the Pillar says, "we just want to pass through."

"No can do." The machine gun man roars with laughter again, followed by the same mockery from a few others, farther beyond the mushrooms. It's the kind of pretentious laugh all cartoonish evil villains have in movies. "Or I will shoot you like this man." He points at the man on the floor who thinks he is a bottle of milk.

Then something horrible happens.

Something that makes living in this world too hard to understand. The machine gun man shoots the man on the ground, blood spilling all over the mushrooms around us.

The Pillar fakes a smile.

I try not to pee my pants. Only for a second. Then I see the men take a selfie with the dead man.

The Pillar's face tenses, as if telling me to hold it together.

But I can't. I am scared mindless.

Then something even stranger happens.

I burst into laughter. The kind of laughter that hurts in the stomach and makes it harder to listen to what others are saying.

The Pillar stares at me with fiery eyes. He's even tenser now. I haven't seen him this angry at me before. "Hold yourself together."

"Why?" I barely mouth the words between my hiccupping episodes of laughter. "I feel good. Really good. Tararara!"

"I get it. It's the mushrooms," the Pillar leans over and whispers. "They affect your brain, like I told you. But you seem to be too sensitive to the effect."

"Mushrooms!" I find myself hailing. I grab one and give it a big smoochy kiss. Then hug it. Then snuggle it.

As I do, I see the stars in the sky have turned into diamonds. So awesome!

I'm Alice in the sky of diamonds.

"What's wrong with your daughter?" the machine gun man grunts.

Did he just shoot bees from between his teeth? I can't stop myself. I start chasing the bees flying around in Mushroomland.

"She's not my daughter." The Pillar purses his lips. He's pissed at me. I know it. But you know what? I love the mushrooms' effect. Because I don't freakin' care. "Don't pay attention to her."

"I'm beginning to lose my patience," the machine gun man says. "You don't know the password, and your daughter is a lunatic."

"I told you she isn't my daughter," I hear the Pillar say while I'm trying to catch a diamond from the sky. "And I don't know the answer to your puzzle. Divide a loaf by a knife? What kind of mathematical question is that?"

"Wrong answer." The man is about to shoot the Pillar while I'm chasing stars.

This is when I find myself standing before the Pillar to protect him. "You will not shoot my father!" I have no idea what I am saying, or why I am saying it. It's strange that in the middle of my hallucination I care for the Pillar.

"Tell her to move, or I will shoot you both," the machine gun man warns.

Then another totally bonkers thing happens. This time it's too insane to swallow.

"Tell you what? You look like you're itching to shoot someone today," the Pillar says, pushing me away toward the man. "Why not shoot her, and let me pass?"

Suddenly, I am two feet away from the machine gun itself, unable to determine if what I just heard was part of my hallucination or for real.

My attempt to turn back and confront the Pillar goes out the window when the machine gun man decides he's had it with me.

He shoots me straight in the chest.

Chapter 12

Buckingham Palace, London

Margaret Kent told the Queen about the mayhem her employees had been ravishing the world with for some time. More Wonderlanders all over the world were secretly planted like sleeper cells among governments, and they were doing a good job.

All in all, the Queen's men and women were making sure the world was going more and more insane.

"Well, I'm not satisfied," The Queen pouted. "More. More. More. I want every child to become an orphan. Every mother to become childless. Every father to lose his family. I don't care if it's contradictory. Just find a way to do it." She strolled all over the place. "I want fascism. Oh, I love that. I want every human to hate another human for being different. Not just color or nationality. I want those with crooked noses to hate those with round noses. Those who have mustaches to hate those who don't. Do you understand?"

Margaret nodded and scribbled something down in her notebook:

Once this is all over and I get the keys, I will kill you, you stupid short and stuffed thing!

"Did you write it down?"

"Of course, My Queen."

"But you can't overdo it." The Queen confused Margaret again. "The idea is to create enough chaos without turning the world into a chaotic place."

"I am not sure I follow you, My Queen."

"That's because you're stupid, Margaret. Ugly and stupid."

I am going to rip you apart when this is over. Chop off your head and roll it all over every soccer field in the world.

"People have to see the world tumble all around them, but stay safe at the same time. Why? Because if we kill everyone, who's going to pay the taxes, buy our products, and ask us to protect them? The key is to scare the citizens, enough to make them need us. And that's when I will rule the world the same way I ruled Wonderland."

Margaret squinted, listening to the Queen. It actually made sense. What was the point of everyone in the world living in pain? They needed a few wars and hassles here and there, so the others, believing the need for them, would simply do as they said.

It had been very much the Queen's philosophy since the Wonderland days, until Alice arrived.

"Understood, My Queen. Anything else?"

"Yes, I just saw a documentary about that short man with the short mustache and short fuse of a temper." She clicked her fingers together. "What was his name again? Charlie Chaplin?"

"Ah, very funny man. What about him?"

"Funny? No, then it's not him. The man I'm talking about was going to kill everyone in the world."

"Uh-huh," Margaret said. "You mean Hitler."

"Yes, that obnoxious little troll. I love him! Can we wake him up? I think he will fit into my plans."

"Hitler is dead, My Queen."

"Unfortunate," the Queen said. "I'd have sworn he was a Wonderland Monster."

"Speaking of Wonderland Monsters," Margaret had to interrupt. "I have been trying to tell you about the new monster for a while, and you just don't want to listen."

"Not again, Margaret. Find me a flamingo that can sing instead. I am in the mood for music."

"I think you should watch this." Margaret turned on the TV.

All of a sudden the Queen shrieked when she saw the Lewis Carroll man on the news. "What?" she neared the screen. "This isn't happening."

"Like I said, I've been trying to tell you all day."

"Is he real?" The Queen's face flushed with fear.

"It's him."

"But he should be dead."

"He isn't."

"Oh, my." The Queen clamped her hands over her mouth. "This can't be happening."

Chapter 13

Okay. So I am dying.

Why am I falling deep through the mud into a pool of marshmallows underground?

And how come fish are swimming inside the mud?

Those mushrooms have really messed me up. I have no idea what's going on.

Sinking deep into a marshmallow abyss, I see the Pillar far beyond the translucent mud, arguing with the machine gun man. When they talk, bubbles foam out of their mouths.

This is so trippy.

I'm Alice underground in the marshmallow water world. I'm Alice who may not be Alice. Hello, nice to meet you. Where have you been? How long am I going to keep sinking?

"Alice!" The Pillar's voice shakes me from the inside.

"Yes?" I manage to say—or have I? It could be all in my mind.

"You must know the answer to this puzzle," the Pillar says.

"The Wonderland mathematics puzzle?" I think I said that. How am I talking beneath the sea of marshmallows?

"Yes. What do you get when you divide a loaf with a knife?"

Suddenly, there is this aching pop in my ears.

"I know the answer!" I raise a hand like a student in a class.

The pop in my ears blew off the pressure in my head. The effect of the mushrooms all around me, I guess. I am back in the real world.

Running my palm all over my chest, I realize I wasn't shot. Not with marshmallows or real bullets.

Sneaky mushrooms.

"That's some wickedly mad daughter you have here," the machine gun man tells the Pillar. "So what's the answer? I don't have all day."

"In Carrollian terms, if you divide a loaf by a knife you get," I say, "bread and butter."

"Right answer!" the machine gun man cheers.

The Pillar raises an eyebrow at me.

"What?" I shake my shoulders. "It's lame, but it's Lewis Carroll. And don't ask me how I know. I just remembered it. I think the real question is how those lowlife gangsters use Lewis Carroll's puzzles as passwords."

"Shut your mouth, girl." The machine gun man is provoked. "You and your father are good to go."

"About time," the Pillar sighs, grabbing my hand.

"You'll meet other gangs on the Mushroom Trail. Good luck with that." The machine gun man says behind us.

I am trying my best to stay focused as the mushrooms grow bigger all around me. "You're sure of this Executioner we're risking our lives for?"

"I'm sure. He definitely knows who cooked the plague." The Pillar clears the way through the thick mushrooms. "Can't you see what the mushrooms are doing to you already?"

"Why aren't you as affected, then?"

"The substance I've been smoking in my hookah for years. It gives me immunity."

"You sound like you've been preparing to come here for a long time."

"Sort of." The Pillar chugged through the darkness. "I'd stop asking questions if I were you. The mushrooms' effects aren't just in your brain. It's like a sleeping poison. If you don't drink from the Executioner's special coconuts in less than an hour, you'll..."

"I will what?" I fold my drugged arms before me.

"You will die, Alice. Why do you think no one outlives the Mushroom Trail unless they meet the Executioner?"

Chapter 14

An abandoned church in London

The Lewis Carroll man entered the abandoned church among his few silent followers, sitting and waiting in silence.

Outside the church the world was getting worse by the minute. What had started with red bubbles had now escalated to furious anger on the verge of violence. So many people were getting in fights that there wasn't enough room in jail for anyone. Some individuals were burning cars and houses, and others were blocking all traffic intersections in London.

Lewis closed the church's door behind him, a smirk stretching from cheek to cheek.

He turned around, walking to the podium while his followers clapped their hands.

"We love you!"

Lewis got to the podium and turned to face his followers. He looked terrible. He hadn't slept for days, and that headache was killing him.

"I-I kn-know you all have it in your heart. A good thing, that is," he began. His voice was soothing and relatable. He'd used to lure tens of children with it in the past. Sometimes he imagined his voice seeping through the paper of his Alice in Wonderland books. "It's not an easy task to believe in the end of the world like you do."

"The world has to end!" an old woman with a cane spat out.

"It's about time!" another middle-aged man cheered.

"I know. I know," Lewis said. "Those people outside have no idea what's happening to them. First they didn't believe me when I told them about the plague. Then they couldn't deny it when they saw its effect on everyone who had bought the Hookah of Hearts last year. And trust me, this is only the beginning."

"We're curious, Lewis," the old woman said. "You say you've been alive all these years. That you were imprisoned in Wonderland. We get that. But what does this plague do to people? Why do they hate each other so much now?"

Lewis smiled inwardly. As if I am going to tell you.

"The plague holds the one virus mankind can't stand," he began. "Revealing it now would spoil the impact of realizing what an awful world this is. But rest assured. Just right before the world really ends, I will tell you what it does to people."

"So why are we gathered here?" another man asked. "You said you wanted us to help you with something."

"Yes, I want you to find me a c..." Suddenly that migraine attacked him again.

Lewis swirled to the floor like a dying hurricane. It'd been so long since the migraine had attacked him this way. Long ago since Wonderland. His head was about to split open. He couldn't take it.

His tongued curled inward. He was choking.

And as he did, he saw himself sinking into muddy ground. Deep down into a sea of mushrooms.

Chapter 15

My feet drag me through the Mushroom Trail.

Never mind my hallucinations. Never mind that I am going to die if I don't get that drink from the Executioner's coconut. I am just a girl trekking her way through a muddy mushroom-infested world, hoping to make sense of it all.

Aren't we all?

"Tell me if the hallucinations increase to a point you're going bonkers," the cigar-smoking Pillar, acting like an older Indiana Jones, tells me.

But what am I supposed to tell him? That I just saw a playing card with legs running next to us in the mud? That when I asked it what it was doing, it told me it was 'playing' because apparently it's a 'playing card'?

No, I don't tell him that. I pretend that never happened.

"In case I die, I need to know how come Lewis Carroll is a Wonderland Monster," I say. "I am sure it's impossible. I met him. He was the sweetest man in the world. I saw him leading the Inklings— which reminds me, why did you buy it for me?"

"Isn't it obvious?" He's pulling a mushroom off its roots to clear a way. "That's your new headquarters in your war against Black Chess. Not everyone has access to the asylum."

"Which reminds me again." I am just babbling whatever comes to mind to forget about the fact that I'm drugged. "Shouldn't it be Black Chess who manufactured the Hookah of Hearts?"

"Not this time. It's the Dodo Corporation," the Pillar says. "And trust me, Black Chess wants to bring chaos to the word, but they don't want to end the world. Who would they rule and manipulate if they killed everyone?"

Then we stop abruptly.

I take a moment, staring at the next obstacle in the road. Or is it just a hallucination of my mind?

I am looking at a man sitting on a desk in the middle of Mushroomland. He is writing feverishly and seems to suffer from a continuous headache.

I am staring at Lewis Carroll—a very shattered and older version of him now, not the one back in London.

Is that the next obstacle in the Mushroom Trail?

Glancing back and forth at the Pillar, I realize he sees this too. Is it possible both of us are hallucinating?

The man raises his head from the writing and stares at us. He smiles, but it isn't a good smile. Not a Lewis Carroll smile.

Then he utters a question the modern world has been asking for more than a century. It's sort of one of the most thought after mysteries of life. "Why do you think a raven is like a writing desk?"

Chapter 16

"Is this real?" I ask the Pillar.

"I'm not sure," The Pillar bites on his cigar.

"Aren't you the one immune to the hallucinations?"

"Not entirely. I am rather sure Lewis Carroll is in London and not here."

"Do you have the answer to his question?"

"Why a raven is like a writing desk?" He lets out some sort of confident pfff. "I'm one of the few who knows the answer."

"So why don't you tell him?"

Just before the Pillar answers me, another group of machine gun men slowly appears from behind the bushes. Those aren't the laughing ones.

"You're here to see the Executioner?" their leader inquires.

"No, we're here to walk on mushrooms," I retort. "Of course we want to see the Executioner, you cuckoo."

The man grimaces, looking at me, anger about to steam out of his ears.

"Don't bother." The Pillar fakes a smile. "She has issues." He spirals his fingers next to his head, indicating I'm mad.

"Issues?" the man says.

"She's just been out of the most secure asylum in London," the

Pillar elaborates. "She ate her warden's left ear. Then the director's right ear. Then she ate the guard's right hand, pulled the left off the guard next to him right off the bat. Plucked her fingers into a taxi driver's nose until he sneezed to death, right before she bit a young man's tongue off like a stretching pastrami. He looked very much like you, by the way."

I wish I could deliver all my lines the way the Pillar does it. The machine gun men take an unconscious step back, steering away from me. The Pillar pulls me closer to him and pats my shoulder. I play along and tuck my thumb into my mouth, flickering my hallucinating eyes at them.

It's funny how each one of us is in his own hallucination world at the moment.

"You will still need to answer a question to pass," the man said. "Not the writing desk question, though."

"Another puzzle." I roll my eyes.

"Shoot," the Pillar says. "Not the gun, but the question."

"What do you do when you find a fork in the road?" the machine gun man says.

"Take the madder road immediately," the Pillar says.

"Wrong answer." The man is ready to shoot us.

Like a lightning strike I spit out the answer. "Take the fork and go find something to eat with it."

The Pillar rolls his eyes now. It's safe to say we've had some considerable amount of eye rolling in the past thirty minutes. It hurts.

"Right answer," the machine gun man says.

The Pillar looks surprised.

I guess my hallucinations are up to par with their melancholic passwords. "What about the man on the writing desk? I thought that was a better puzzle." I tell the machine gun man.

"What man on a writing desk?"

When I look, Lewis Carroll and his famous desk are gone. I glance back at the Pillar. He seems uninterested. "Let's just move on."

"One last thing," the machine gun man says. "This is the last of the Mushroom Trail. Beyond the next few mushrooms, there is an open field."

"Is that where meet the Executioner?" I wonder.

"That is where the drug cartels are in continues war," the man says. "Where everyone dies within a few moments. So sober up."

Carefully, the Pillar and I step closer beyond the mushrooms. Then we part a few smaller ones blocking the view. We could already hear the sound of war. The screaming. The shooting. The tanks rolling heavily on the ground.

Then we see it all.

"A war." The Pillar's cigar dangles from his lips. "So boring. I've seen better on CNN."

But I don't find it boring. It scares me to death. All the blood, gunfire, and screams. I need to find the Executioner and his damn coconut. How am I supposed to survive this war?

Chapter 17

First, a bomb explodes a few feet away from me.

Then there is this flying Columbian dude air-paddling from the explosion in midair. He looks like he's just been shot out of a cannon. A nearby helicopter finishes the dramatic masterpiece and chops off his head with its blades. The head flies off in midair again, lands closer to us, and starts rolling toward me.

"Does this head know it's dead?" the Pillar comments.

Delirious, my feet are cemented in the mud. The Pillar pulls me closer, and we start running. Behind us, the helicopter crashes exactly where we once stood, right over that poor head.

Fire guns, wind, and shotguns are everywhere.

I run, pant, holding the Pillar's hand. I am very much upset with myself. But I am not myself anymore. The mushrooms are messing with my head, and it's hard to tell what is going on. All I know is that I need the Executioner's coconut—as silly and preposterous as it sounds.

"Duck, Alice." The Pillar pulls me down as a missile churns through the air, right into a Jeep.

"What are they fighting for?" I ask.

"They're fighting over the throne of the mushroom empire all around the world. They grow it here, sell it for millions. But the question is who rules this jungle?"

"The Executioner, I suppose?"

"I thought so, too," the Pillar says. "He was the main drug supplier in Wonderland, but it seems he can hardly get a grip on this real world."

"So how do we find him?"

"I have a feeling I'm going to steal that Jeep with the dead men in it. It looks functional," he says. "You don't mind riding alongside the dead. Do you?"

We duck and run like scurrying rats along the fields, pushing our luck and hoping not to get shot by a wandering bullet or a missile.

I see a man on top of a missile, riding it like a banana boat, saying hooray!

Happens all the time, I tell myself.

"How come everyone enjoys murdering each other?" I ask the Pillar.

"Humankind, dear Alice, have enjoyed that sport since Cain and Abel." He jumps into the Jeep, and I follow. "Luckily, killing is prohibited these days, unless you do it en masse. They call it conquering."

"So I'm supposed to accept living in such a bloody world?" I shout against the maddening sound of war, then pull a dead body out of the passenger's seat.

"No Alice, you're supposed to outlive it," The Pillar ignites the ramshackle Jeep and chugs through the mist of smoke and bullets.

"Stop that," I protest, as the Jeep bumps over a few dead bodies. "Always trying to pose the human race as a bunch of lunatic apes who'll never learn to love and live with one another."

"In spite of this not being the time or place to have this conversation, I'd like to point out that advertisers pay tenfold for TV ads when the news is covering major war disasters around the world. Now duck before that bullet hits you and you make the news."

I feel so dizzy. I can't even pull out my umbrella and shoot at anyone.

Wait. Why do I suddenly feel so aggressive, wanting to shoot people? The mushrooms must be doing this to me.

"Hey!" The Pillar points at a dying soldier reaching out at us. He's holding a letter in one hand.

Amidst the impossible killing fields, the Pillar detours closer to the soldier and pulls the letter from his hands.

"Send it to my family," the soldier pleads. "Tell them I love them, and that I've buried over a hundred thousand dollars of drug money in the back yard."

"Nah, I'm not taking that letter," the Pillar says. " You should have sent them an SMS. Twitter post? You know you can schedule those, right? Maybe schedule the to the day of your death?" The Pillar tucks the letter in his pocket. "Besides, who writes letters anymore? Die, you old-fashioned typewriter!"

I don't comment because I'm not sure this is really happening.

But then something assures me I'm not hallucinating this war at all. Every bit of this is real. Someone has shot me in my left arm.

Chapter 18

"**C**ongratulations," the Pillar says. "You can brag now that you went to war."

"Why isn't it hurting?" I stare at my bleeding arm.

"It's just a scratch." He is smiling broadly. "You're not really hit. Let's see if there is music in this car. Take the wheel."

I take the wheel with my right hand because I can't move my left arm.

Then Pink Floyd plays on the radio. Comfortably Numb is the song.

The Pillar tucks the cigar back into his mouth and continues driving like a tourist on safari watching the wildlife. I'm stunned at his ability to avoid bullets and missiles.

All until a tank bangs into our Jeep from the side.

As the Jeep rolls over, half of it under the tank already, I realize how much I'm drugged now. I need that coconut.

The world upside down doesn't look much different from the normal world. Or maybe that's how all fields of war look.

I lie on my back, listening to men jumping out of their Jeeps. They pull me up, grab me by my hands, never mind my achy, screaming left arm, and pull me toward their leader. The Pillar is pulled next to me.

We stop at one point and are ordered to raise our injured heads to stare at their leader.

I see a well-built man with a long scar on his right cheek sitting on top of the tank. He is overly sunburned. And of all things, he has his legs crossed and he is smoking a hookah atop of a mushroom in the middle of this war.

"What is a girl like you doing here in Mushroomland?" he says in a most foreign accent.

"I—" My eyelids droop as I am trying to stay awake. "I'm looking for the Executioner."

The man stops smoking. "Is that so?" He rubs his chin. "And why would you be looking for him?"

"I need his coconut drink to survive the Mushroom Trail." I can't believe we're talking with all this mess of killing still going on all around us.

"You walked the Mushroom Trail?" He doesn't laugh or show emotion. I've rarely met a man I am so afraid of. He's exuding a vague sinister personality I haven't seen before.

"It's a long story," I say. "Please lead to me to the Executioner."

"You know what they say about the Executioner?" He pulls out a Magnum .45, loads it, and then points it at me. "That you can meet him only once. You know why?"

I start to realize I am talking to the Executioner himself.

"Because you only look at me once, and then you have to die." The Executioner aims his pistol at me with a smirk on his face. This time I think it's real.

"Wait." The Pillar wakes up from his fall. "Don't shoot the girl. It's me."

The Executioner slowly turns his head. The Pillar is covered in dust, so it makes sense not to recognize him right away. But why would he recognize the Pillar in the first place? I am confused.

"Carter Chrysalis Cocoon Pillar!" The Executioner squints at the professor. "Is that you?"

"In the flesh." The Pillar tucks what's left of his cigar in his mouth.

I am baffled. I'm Alice's all lost and delirious thoughts mixed in a bag of mushrooms and M&M's.

The Executioner gets off his mushroom and stares at the Pillar with wonder. It might be my mistake, but the look in his eyes is that of a man fascinated with the Pillar. "Is that really you, Pillardo?"

Pillardo?

The Pillar mumbles something in Columbian, and the two men embrace like old friends.

"You know him?" Sorry, but I have to ask. I mean, what the mushy mushrooms is going on?

"Know him?" The Executioner raises an eyebrow. "Who doesn't know Senor Pillardo, the most legendary drug lord of all time?"

Chapter 19

Radcliffe Lunatic Asylum, Oxford

Dr. Tom Truckle could not believe what he saw on national TV. People had come out on every street in London to stir all kinds of chaos.

He saw a man in his underwear with a baseball bat chasing his family out on the streets. Another maniac woman had gone into an unexplained episode of road rage, chasing her co-workers with her damaged car. The owner of Tom's favorite soup shop had locked everyone inside, confessing to serving them frogs and now forcing them to drink his soup until they puked.

Tom watched the BBC's TV host, and her crew abandon their camera and run away, leaving it to record all of the mayhem.

This must be the end of days, Tom thought. He hadn't dared switch on the channel to take a look at what was happening in America or the rest of the world.

What troubled him deeply was everyone in Oxford had gone just as mad, which suggested his asylum was in danger now.

"Lock up the asylum!" Tom shouted at his guards. "And by that, I mean use the Plan-X system."

"Are you sure you want to do that?" the guard asked on the other side.

"I am sure. The time has come to lock every one of us within these steel walls inside," Tom said.

Running down the stairs, he entered the underground ward and walked among the Mushroomers on both sides. They were panicking, afraid of the world outside. Tom couldn't help but remember all of the Pillar's warnings about the world outside the asylum, how they were the real mad ones, not the Mushroomers.

"You're going to be okay," Tom tried to calm them down, looking for Waltraud.

"We want Alice!" the Mushroomers said.

Tom had no idea what to tell them. Alice and the Pillar had left on one of their crazy missions. As much as he loathed them both, he also felt sorry for them, having to deal with the mad world outside.

"Waltraud," Tom called upon seeing her, mushing the brains out of a patient. "Stop whatever you're doing."

"Why?" she said in her German accent.

"Why?" he roared at her, his hands reaching for his pills already. "Apocalypse is why! The world is ending outside. I am issuing Plan-X. We're closing all doors and will self-contain ourselves inside."

"But—"

"Stop interrupting me! I'm only waiting for my children to arrive, and then the doors will seal shut. I want you to order our people in the kitchen to open up all the reserve refrigerators and start pulling out all food and supply."

Plan-X had been the asylum's contingency strategy since long ago. Actually, it had been Tom's father's idea. The old man, now in his grave, had predicted the end of the world long ago. Thus, the asylum was pre-prepared with food and living supplies for one year on.

And the time has come father, Tom thought.

But Waltraud Wagner stiffened in her place. She couldn't pull her eyes off the TV. Something about what was happening outside seemed to appeal to her.

Tom had no time to argue with her. He should have shoved her in a cell long ago. After all, he'd only hired her because she had killed her own patients back in the day, when she was a nurse in Vienna.

Tom turned to the bald Ogier and ordered him to speak to the people in the kitchen.

Ogier nodded obediently and issued the process.

"Don't worry," Tom addressed the panicking Mushroomers. "You will be safe in here." He couldn't believe he'd just said those words. Never had he loved the Mushroomers, but with the world going down in flames outside, he saw how weak they were. He suddenly began to relate to them.

Then Tom remembered something he'd forgotten upstairs. Two stairs at a time, he dashed into the VIP ward, finally standing before the flamingo's cell.

"I couldn't leave you alone," Tom said, wondering why his heart began softening toward the animal. Maybe it was the end of the world's effect on him.

He pulled the cell's door open and let the flamingo out.

"You have two options," he told it. "Go back to your Queen in the mad world outside or stay with us...well, in the mad world inside."

It was clear the flamingo wanted to stay, but it also looked puzzled, as if awaiting an answer from Tom.

"Okay," Tom waved a hand. "I will tell you one of my biggest secrets, and I will only tell you."

The flamingo's eyes bulged out with curiosity.

"I'm not who you think I am, but I will not tell you about it, at least not now." Tom swallowed another pill. "What I can tell you is that I was told about this by my father long ago. He called it the last days before the War. And by this, I mean he told me about the end of times, the appearance of the Wonderland Monsters, the end of the world, and how to build a safe house, a bunker to survive it. Only I was asked to disguise it as an asylum and gather as many mad people as I could, because those are the ones who're going to save the world."

Chapter 20

Mushroomland, Columbia

"**Y**ou're a drug lord?" I can't believe it.

"Semantics. I prefer the term Professor Feelgood." The Pillar hands over the coconut drink. "Sip it slowly. It will take an hour or two before the mushrooms' effect wears off."

I hesitate taking it from him.

"Come on. It's not poisoned. I won't hurt you."

I'm not really sure of that, but I have no choice. If I don't drink it, I'll die.

It's actually not just that. Since I heard about the Pillar being a drug lord, I've had the unexplained urge to shoot him dead. I don't know why I feel so aggressive. It could be the hallucinations.

Maybe all this world really needs is to get rid of the Pillar.

"So Senor Pillardo"—the Executioner guides us into his missile-proof Humvee—"let's go back to my castle. We have a lot to talk about."

"Actually, I'm running out of time..."

"Trust me, we have a lot of time—and drugs and mushrooms. And hookahs. And girls. All you need, like in the old days," the Executioner says. "I understand that you didn't just come here to see me. We know that is definitely not the case.".

For the first time ever, I see the Pillar lower his gaze, just a little. What is going on between those two?

"I promise I will look into whatever you need to talk about, but first we have to enjoy some time in my castle. Just like the old days, Senior. Remember those? Man, you were some psycho maniac back then, but you sure made the deals of the century selling drugs, and a lot of money."

My hands slide down and reach for my umbrella. What if I just shoot both of them? Wouldn't the world be a better place?

Entering the Humvee, we watch the world burn in flames behind us as we're driving to the Executioner's castle.

"So what's this war all about?" I ask. "Aren't you all friends here, selling mushrooms?"

"I think Senor Pillardo can tell you himself." The Executioner laughs.

The Pillar takes a moment then returns to his sarcasm. "It's nothing. The Executioner's boys are having fun. Killing for sport."

The Executioner eyes the Pillar. "Ah, so you don't want to tell her?" He turns to me. "Let me tell you why my men are killing each other, little girl. But right after we have some drinks in my castle."

"We don't have time for your damn castle!" Is it the drugs? Is it me? "We came for..."

The Executioner pulls out another machine gun, a bigger one this time, and points it at me. I'm starting to get bored of this. If you're going to point a gun, better use it. "I really don't like shooting." His sinister intentions show through now. "We're going to have a welcome meal, then I will listen to what both of you want with me, and then I will decide whether I will kill you or not."

Chapter 21

The Executioner's castle looks as if it was cut from the pages of a fairy tale, except the part with the guards and their machine guns. It's hard to believe this man lives in such an expensive mansion while enjoying the world burning all around him. I'm still not over this dark world I have been thrown into. But I can't do anything about it before the mushrooms' effect wears off completely.

I don't want to end up spreading violence to an already violent reality, and then figure out later I had a chance to bring some peace into the world with a little patience instead.

Crossing the lush landscape full of hedges shaped after Wonderland characters, the Executioner informs me he had the March Hare design it for him. "I had to put my business on halt for two months and inject him with a hallucinogen so he wouldn't know who I was," he explained. "The March with his naive child-like attitude wouldn't have designed it if he knew who I was."

"And who are you, really?" I pretend I have given in to his reality.

"I'm the Executioner, like in the Alice books. I used to work for the Queen to chop off heads, but now I've gone solo, and trust me, she fears me more that anything else."

"So you're just another Wonderland Monster."

The Executioner laughs again, entering the vast entrance of his castle. The architecture looks like something from a thousand and one nights.

"That's not an answer," I say.

"It's not meant to be," he replies without looking at me, then sits himself on his throne in the middle of a sky-lit hall.

"What a fabulous job you did to the castle." The Pillar, cigar in mouth, admires the place. "I feel like I'm in Taj Mahal."

"I'm humbled," the Executioner says. "Senor Pillardo himself compliments me."

"What happened to the horses?" the Pillar asks.

"Sorry, senior. They all died after you left. I tried to be nice to them, but they kept kicking my men, looking for you. I had to shoot them all," the Executioner says, pouring himself a pink drink. "We built a casino where your horses used to live. Very profitable, but nobody goes there anymore. It's too crowded."

The Pillar grins. "How does no one go there anymore if it's too crowded?"

I sense it's not a question, but some kind of an inside joke.

"It's Wonderland logic," the Executioner explains to me. "It's like saying: it ain't over until it's over." He hands the Pillar a drink.

"Ah, I remember those." The Pillar sips his drink. "I remember when we used to say: always go to other people's funerals, otherwise they won't go to yours."

The Executioner is amused. "I loved that phrase. Because if you went to their funeral, they were dead already." He turns to me with a smile. "I bet your friend here hasn't seen the Wonderland days."

"Be careful." The Pillar winks. "She thinks she is Alice. The Real one."

This throws the Executioner off. "Oh, my." He chuckles. "That's a new one." He turns to me again. "Alice is dead, darling. True, we can't remember what she looked like, but she's dead."

Just when I am about to ask why he's so sure, a horde of young and skinny children are brought into the castle, wearing tattered clothes, dirt sticking to their sunburned skin.

"What now?" The Executioner pouts at the man who brought them in.

"I thought you'd like to see that we cut their fingers like you asked us." the man says.

My eyes flip, staring at the children's bandaged hands. They cut their fingers? What the hell?

"Two knuckles from each kid," the man says. "Just like you always demand. Should I send them to the field now?"

My anger chokes me up. I turn and stare at the Pillar. He signals for me to stay cool and hush it down. I will explain later, he mouths.

But damn it, I won't stay cool. Who is this horrible Executioner? I was right when I thought of ridding the world of him.

Chapter 22

"I want you to find this Lewis Carroll and bring him to me," the Queen roared at Margaret. "Now!"

"How am I supposed to do that, My Queen? You know what kind of a monster he is."

"Just figure it out!" The Queen padded the chamber left and right, hands behind her back. "It's too soon for an apocalypse. I want a mad world. Not a dead world. Besides, why is he here? What does he want with the end of the world?"

"I have no idea, but what you're asking me isn't something I can do," Margaret says. "Normally I'd use the Cheshire's help with something like that, but he made it clear he isn't on our side. He just wants to bring chaos into the human world for his own giggles and grins. I wouldn't be surprised if he's in this with Lewis Carroll."

"Then the Pillar is our only chance," the Queen says. "Where is he?"

"Haven't seen him since the last time when I visited this Alice girl to convince her she should be one of us," Margaret said. "I met him briefly afterward, trying to get the key from him, but he said he'd like to keep it until we find the next one. Sort of a guarantee, so nothing bad happens to him until we both fulfill our sides of the deal."

"I know how to get the key from the Pillar later, that's hardly my problem," the Queen said. "Don't mention it to him now. Just find him, and ask for his help. He has his own out-of-this-world methods. He should be able to stop this Wonderland Monster."

"I will look for him right away, My Queen." Margaret was checking her phone. "Wait, I just received information: he took Alice and flew all the way to Columbia?"

The Queen stopped. "Columbia?" She tilted her head. "You're thinking what I am thinking?"

"The Executioner?" Margaret spelled out slowly.

"It makes sense. Whoever designed this plague in the hookahs must be related to the Executioner. It's where all the hallucinogens are cooked." The Queen rubbed her chin.

"So the Pillar is looking for a cure in Columbia?"

"I hope that's all he is looking for," the Queen said. "I hope he isn't digging into the past, or this will have dire consequences. What kind of complicated day is today?" She romped her feet on the ground.

"Today is Sunday, My Queen."

"Here's my second request to the Parliament," she said, chin up. "No more Sundays!"

"That's impossible. It's an important day to the people."

"No, it's not. I haven't been cool with the days of the week being seven anyways. God made the world in six days. And Lewis Carroll, when he was still sane, thought about six impossible things for breakfast. And we're looking for six keys. Now six weekdays feels about right."

"Whatever you say, My Queen." Margaret chewed on the words.

"So, back to our problem. Send someone to follow the Pillar in Columbia."

"You're aware that very few Wonderlanders have the guts to go there, right? Not even me or the Cheshire."

"Then find those who have the guts. Wasn't Wonderland full of gory loons? Find one and send them after the Pillar to expedite his search for a cure."

"I need to make some phone calls," Margaret said and left the chamber.

The Queen turned and stared into the mirror. "What are you doing, Pillar?" she mumbled. "Are you planning on opening those old wounds from the past again?"

Chapter 23

Mushroomland, Columbia

Gritting my teeth, I watch the poor kids being led outside.

"Where are they going?" I ask, my hands trembling.

"None of your business, little girl," the Executioner says. "I'm starting to lose my patience with you."

"Why not have another drink?" the Pillar interrupts.

Oh, God. How I hate both of them.

"Indeed." The Executioner pours more of the pink liquid. "And since you're in the mood for more drinks, here is what I will do. I know you have a question you want to ask me."

"Finally," I hiss.

"Yes," the Pillar says. "I'm looking for a cure for the Hookah of Hearts plague that's sweeping over the world by the minute—suspiciously enough, it has no effect on this region of the world."

"Oh, that."

"I know you don't care about the world outside of Mushroomland, but I really need to stop the plague," the Pillar says.

"I saw it on TV this morning," the Executioner says. "Very funny plague. Did you see the naked teacher on the bicycle chasing his wife, trying to kill her?"

"Haven't had the pleasure," the Pillar says.

"Well... I understand it's Lewis Carroll who spread the disease," the Executioner considers. "I have to admit I don't want to have anything to do with him. You know how mad and angry he can get, with all those migraines of his."

I can't believe they're talking about Lewis Carroll, but finding the cure is my priority now. I don't say a word.

"I know," the Pillar says, "but we need the cure."

"The thing is, there is no cure, Senor Pillardo."

"You're sure about that?"

"I'm sure because you have no idea what the hookahs do to people."

"It turns them into nuts, just like the mushrooms did to me," I say.

"That's an understatement to the brilliance of what this plague really does to people." The Executioner taps the diamond grail he is drinking from. "This plague does something to people you would never have imagined in a million years. And once you realize what it is, you'll understand why there is no cure."

"What does it do?" I demand.

"Like I said, I'm not saying because I don't want to have anything to do with Lewis Carroll." The Executioner stands up. "But I know who cooked it for him."

"That's a start." The Pillar steps forward. "Who?"

"I'm not telling you that either." The Executioner smirks. "Not until you entertain me like in the old days, Senor Pillardo. Come on, make me laugh."

The Pillar stiffens for a fraction of a second. "Of course." He raises his glass. "Want to play Wonderland logic again?"

"Whatever's on your mind. Just be sure you make me laugh." The Executioner hands him a pistol. "And for starters, I laugh when someone shoots one of my guards. How about that for a start?"

"My pleasure." The Pillar grabs the gun from the table and shoots two of the guards without hesitation.

I swallow hard and step away from him. Never have I imagined him this cruel. But who am I kidding? He has twelve dead people on his conscience.

"Frabjous! Haven't lost your swift speed, Senor Pillardo." The Executioner clinks glasses with the Pillar. "Now make me really laugh. Tell me jokes. Tell me about your adventures outside of Mushroomland all of these years. But I have to warn you, if you don't make me laugh..."

"You will shoot me and the girl, I know."

"No." The Executioner approaches him. "I will make you shoot one of those kids outside, make the girl watch it, and then shoot you and her."

This is the moment when I raise my trembling hand, unable to stay here any longer. "Is there a bathroom nearby?"

"Just outside that door, to the left," The Executioner says dismissively. He is so much into the Pillar.

I turn and leave. Not for the bathroom. But for the children. It might be close to the end of the world, but I'm finding those children and getting them out of Mushroomland, if it's the last thing I do before judgement day.

Chapter 24

Outside, I don't bother finding the bathroom. I just want out to look for the children.

Among the Executioner's soldiers, I pretend I am an airhead brat with a colorful umbrella, trekking around the vast landscape and admiring the roses.

Some of them are irritated by me, borderline offended, but none of them can do anything about it. I have the Executioner's permission to be out here.

Flashing my stupid-girl smiles, I'm looking for the children in my peripheral vision.

Nighttime isn't helping much. All I have for light is a small moon up in the sky. For a moment, it looks like a mushroom lighting up the world. But I know better. The coconut's effect hasn't fully worked on me yet.

Farther into the landscape, I am happy to be hiding between folds of darkness and even darker trees in the castle's garden. I am like a cat now. I see everyone from my vantage point but none of them see me. The Cheshire comes to mind instantly, but I don't want to think about him.

Then I glimpse the children in the distance.

They're being loaded like sheep into a barred Jeep, surrounded by machine gun men.

Like a cat, I tiptoe closer. Each child is given a gun before getting on the Jeep. Oh, my God.

I mean, I've read about drug lords and cartels using young, poor children in their drug business, even in war, but I never thought I'd see it with my own eyes. It seems that the words we read in newspapers, the videos we watch on news cable, no matter how atrocious and unbelievable are never really processed by our brains. We watch these things as if they are a movie, as if they're not real, until you see them with your own eyes.

But right now, I can't stand it. Those children aren't going to become machine gun drug traffickers. Their childhood isn't going to be taken advantage of by this mean man called the Executioner. I will find a way to get them out of Mushroomland.

This means more to me than the end of the world.

Because frankly, the world will end anyway. It's the crimes we don't do anything about that are the real evil.

Chapter 25

Taking my shoes off, I pad as slowly as I can, closer to the Jeep.

There are about twenty children, and for some reason, they're shown out of the Jeep again. One of the machine gun men tells them to wait next to a huge mushroom tree—haven't seen one before, really, but hey, I could still be imagining things.

Once the kids are alone, I approach them, worried they'll shoot or resist me because I'm foreign or something.

But they don't.

They actually look at me as if they know me, anticipating whatever I have to say.

"I'm Alice," I begin. "I will get you out of here. You want to get out of here, right?"

They nod eagerly, and I realize they don't speak my language, but they seem to understand me, still. Maybe freedom and children's rights is a universal thing. No language is really needed.

"Look," I try to explain things with my hands while I talk. Common sense sign language should work, right? "I don't know what I'm going to do, but how about you all get into that Jeep again. I can drive it away until we figure out what to do next."

They follow my pointing finger to the Jeep, guns still in their hands.

"No," I say. "No guns. You don't need them."

They're reluctant about it, but cooperate eventually. One after the other they get into the Jeep, smiling at me. It's lovely how a child's smile makes your life seem worthless in order to save them.

But it's not funny at all seeing each one of them is missing knuckles on their last two fingers, starting from the pinky. I can't explain how this breaks my heart. I suddenly feel embarrassed complaining about shock therapy back in the asylum. At least no one cut off a piece of me.

"Hey." I stop a boy and kneel down to face him. "Who did that to you?" I point at the missing fingers.

"The Executioner." Of course.

"Why?"

"Mark."

"Mark?" I blink. "Who's Mark?"

"No." The boy waves his forefinger. "Slave. Mark."

My hands reach for my mouth to cup a shriek. "It's a mark? Like a tattoo? You're a salve?"

"Executioner slave." The boy taps his chest and then points to the rest of the children. "Travel. Drug. Sell."

"Not anymore." I hug him closer. "I will take care of you."

The boy smiles broadly, as if I have bought him a gift. I mean, God, he doesn't even know what they are doing to him, trapped within the walls of mushroom all around.

Before he gets in the Jeep, he turns around and touches my hair. "Alice," he whispers. "Mother say Alice come. Alice save us."

Chapter 26

Inside the Jeep, lights still out, I try to think of a plan.

So what? I am going to ignite the vehicle with the kids inside and just try to escape Mushroomland?

It doesn't really sound like a plan, and now that I've given the children hope, it really doesn't sound like a plan.

"Think, Alice." I bang my hands on the wheel, staring at the machine gun men in the distance. It'll only be minutes before they come back.

My hatred for the Pillar increases. Or maybe I should blame myself for counting too much on him. Who was I fooling? I wasn't the least bit surprised when I learned he was a drug lord. I bet he marked children like the Executioner does. That bastard.

I fiddle with my umbrella, realizing it only has a few bullets. I can go back to put one in the Executioner and then another in the Pillar, but what good will that do for the children?

Suddenly, one of the machine gun men sees us and blows red fireworks in the sky, exposing the Jeep for everyone to see.

It's too late now for a plan. Survival instinct at its core.

I push the pedal and bump into every hedge and mushroom in my way, trying to chug my way out of here.

Jeeps start following me, shooting at us.

Now I'm worried one of the kids will get hurt. I ask them to duck, but for how long?

Farther I drive, my hands gripping the wheel, my brain still foggy.

Alice save us. Had the boy's mother predicted my arrival, like Constance believed in me?

What do you do when everyone believes in you, and deep down inside you know you're insane?

I take a left onto an even muddier road. The Jeep slows down. But I am not stopping. I grip the wheel harder, grit my teeth as I push the pedal against its capacity.

But it's not the chasing that stops me. It's the flaring white light someone directs in my face.

I end up seeing nothing, only feeling the weight of the Jeep rolling on its side. My head bumps into something, and all I end up with is the aching sound of the wheels circling the air.

Are the children hurt?

It's only a minute before I see the Executioner looking down on me. "I should have killed you once I saw you." He pulls his gun out again.

Next to him, the Pillar's face comes into focus. His face is inanimate. And for the first time, I can see his real intentions. His eyes are so dead I don't think he ever cared for me one bit.

He tucks his cigar back in his mouth and says, "Love that look on someone's face, just before they die."

Chapter 27

Westminster Palace, Margaret Kent's Office

Margaret stood in front of her favorite mirror in her office, checking out her face. She wanted to see if her surgeons, who'd cost her a fortune, had messed up anything in her operation.

But on the contrary, everything was just fine.

The face she'd asked for to cover up her ugliness, and put her Duchess days behind, was like nothing she'd ever seen. In fact, she loved how she looked. It suited her prestige and made people trust her—which was most crucial to her title in the Parliament.

Then why did the Queen of Hearts keep calling her ugly?

Margaret looked away from the mirror and out at the River Thames. She knew why the Queen treated her this way. Because she couldn't forget how ugly she was in Wonderland. Because the Queen envied her for being able to pull such a trick in the real world.

The Queen herself had asked the same doctors to make her taller—the Queen's biggest setback. But science in this world only knew how to make extreme makeovers with faces. Making someone taller wasn't an option yet.

How Margaret wished to kill this obnoxious Queen. How she wished to rip her to pieces.

But none of that was feasible before they collected the Six Impossible Keys.

It just had to be done. And now she had to find someone to send after that madman, the Pillar who seemed to be looking for a cure in Columbia.

Never mind that Columbia was the best place to look for those who created this plague, but it was also where Margaret had made most of her fortune.

Margaret had been one of the first to arrive from Wonderland. With her political position, she was able to make millions of pounds by endorsing drug trafficking and child slavery in Columbia.

A very profitable business, indeed.

She worried the Pillar would mess up things there. His travel to Columbia seemed to have a deeper reason behind it. True, he was there to find a cure of sorts, but why go back to that place he hated so much?

Why go back to that dark pit of his past?

Margaret sighed, deciding her priority was to find a cure and keep her assets in Columbia safe. She had to call someone to do it.

She walked back to her desk, and dialed a number. It belonged to the last Wonderlander she'd ever work with, but it seemed that every Wonderlander needed to make a stand now.

Either you were part of Black Chess, or you were an Inklings. There was no other way around it now.

Chapter 28

Mushroomland, Columbia

With the gun's barrel in my mouth, I can only speak in nonsensical vowels.

And even though no one understands me, the Executioner ends up curious to know what I have to say before I die.

"I was only coughing." I wipe the gun's staining powder from my lips. From the corner of my eye, I can see the kids aren't hurt.

The Pillar raises an eyebrow at me, probably impressed with my comeback.

The Executioner loads his gun again, ready to finish me.

"Wait," I say. "Since you're a Wonderlander, you must be looking for the keys like everyone else." My look is sharp and challenging. "The Six Impossible Keys."

The Executioner pulls his gun to a halt. I believe I caught his interest. Behind him, the Pillar scratches his temples.

"Continue..." The Executioner waves the gun at me.

"I know where one of them is," I say, reminding myself I'll never tell about the one key I have hidden in my back pocket. The one Lewis Carroll gave me. "Last week, the Mad Hatter took it from me."

"From you?" The Executioner seems skeptical. "Why would you

have a key to Wonderland?"

"Well." I rub the back of my neck. "Like I said before, I am Alice from Wonderland. I just don't remember a lot of it. I had the key hidden in a bucket in the basement of my family's house."

The Executioner scans me from top to bottom.

"You don't want to kill me, in case I know of the whereabouts of the other keys," I follow up, not sure if the Pillar will back me up if I mention him to the Executioner, so I don't. He wanted me dead a minute ago.

The Executioner gazes back at the Pillar and then back at me. His eyes are sharp, as if he's trying to read through my soul.

It's a long moment. I take advantage of it and smile at the children behind me, assuring them they will be all right.

The moment stretches even more, and I begin to worry the Executioner won't believe me.

But he breaks the long silence with a spitting laugh. His men laugh with him. He lowers his head toward me and says, "You're the maddest girl I have ever seen." He raises his eyebrows. "I love mad people. That's why I will not kill you until I'm thoroughly entertained by your hallucinations."

Chapter 29

The Pillar, me, and the Executioner are sitting around a table in the middle of his garden. I can hear the sounds of war in the distance, still not sure what his men are fighting over.

But the war is the least of my worries now. It's the Executioner and his sadistic games. He literally wants us to play a game now.

"It's a very easy game," he says. "But most entertaining to me."

The Pillar says nothing, and neither do I. The Executioner had each of us hold a gun and place it atop the table, both hands placed palm down.

"Here is how it's going to be played," the Executioner says. "I will ask you a question." He is talking to me. I've become his priority now. He thinks I am mad, and it amuses him. "If you give the right answer, you will pass for this round. If it's wrong, I will shoot you."

"Suspenseful." The Pillar puffs his cigar. "I love suspense."

"Then it'll be your turn to ask me a question." The Executioner is still talking to me. "If I answer it the wrong way, you can shoot me."

"Justice," the Pillar says nonchalantly. "Not a fan."

"Then Senor Pillardo will join in," the Executioner follows. "Easy game. Say the truth and you will live."

"How can you tell I am telling the truth when you ask me?" I say.

"The same way you can tell I am telling the truth when I ask you."

The Executioner grins.

"Nonsense," the Pillar comments. "My favorite."

"I'm not following," I tell the Executioner.

"Here is the thing, young lady," the Executioner says. "This is a game of nonsense—which, if you think you're Alice, you should know a lot about."

"Trust me. Nonsense has been my middle name since I met the Pillar—I mean, Senor Pillardo," I say. "But I still don't have a grip on this game."

"Here is how this game is really played," the Pillar finally interjects "The thing is that all questions asked have only one answer."

I tilt my head, worrying I am not going to grasp this fully.

"All questions in this game are answered by saying 'Hookah Hookah,'" the Pillar explains, his eyes on the Executioner. I am more curious than ever to know whatever is happening between those two. "I ask you, 'How are you?' You answer, 'Hookah Hookah.' I ask you, 'Where have you been?' You say..."

"Hookah Hookah, I get it," I say. "So how is anyone supposed to know if the other is telling the truth?"

The Pillar and the Executioner exchange mean looks for a moment.

"It's how you say it, Alice," the Executioner explains. "If you can convince me with you tonality and facial expressions it's the truth, then it's the truth."

Chapter 30

I don't have enough time to object.

The Executioner demonstrates the game by asking the Pillar, "What's your name?"

"Hookah Hookah," the Pillar says, as if he's just used to answering it this way. It's mind boggling how believable he sounds.

"Where are you from?"

"Hookah Hookah," the Pillar answers with a home-sick expression on his face. I suppose that deeper in his mind he was saying 'Wonderland.'

Then the Executioner turns to face me. "Do you think the Pillar is a good man?"

Now, that's a shocker.

Sneaky. The Executioner just asked the question I'm not sure how to answer. The game demands confidence and truth in the way I say Hookah Hookah.

It takes me a while to answer. "Hookah Hookah."

In my mind, the answer is 'I don't know.' It's the truth. I try my best to sound as if I mean it.

The Executioner's sharp eyes pierce through me, his fingers reaching for his gun.

I shrug.

"Good answer," he says. "I don't know either."

What? He read my mind?

"My turn," I say. "Do you truly believe I will not shoot you without waiting for the next question?"

"Hookah Hookah." He nods toward his guards standing all around us.

Okay. He can actually read my mind. And I am toast because of the guards. But wait!

"But this means that even if I catch you lying in this game, I won't be able to shoot you," I argue. "Because your guards will shoot me first."

"Smart girl," the Executioner says. "In this game, only you or the Pillar will end up dead. Can you see how nonsense always plays in my favor?"

Chapter 31

Somewhere in the streets of London

The mayhem in the streets of London fascinated the Cheshire.

All those lowlife human beings getting in fights with each other, some of them taking it far, as in really hurting one another. That was just fantastic.

He roamed the streets on foot, possessing one person after another and contributing to the madness. A punch in the face here. A tickle there. Setting a place on fire here. It was all fun.

Revenge on humankind felt so sweet he was about to purr like his ancestors once did.

Blood was everywhere on the streets. Traffic had stopped hours ago. This was better than anything he'd ever seen. He wondered what kind of plague it was, but couldn't put his paws on it.

Lewis Carroll turned out to be one mad nut, even crazier than all the rest. How hadn't the Cheshire ever known about this man's crazy tendencies to spread chaos to the world?

But even though he enjoyed possessing a soul after another, it suddenly occurred to him that he had no idea of who *he* really was.

Of course, he was a cat in a way or another. But he'd even lost his recollection of what he looked like as a cat many years ago.

Who was he, really? What did he look like? What was the look that really suited his personality?

Had the Cheshire been lost among the many faces he'd possessed, now that he was just a nobody?

His thoughts were interrupted by a phone call. Yes, he possessed many souls, but always passed on his phone so he'd be in contact with whoever wanted to benefit from his expertise.

Like all cats, the Cheshire needed to make a living.

"It's Margaret," the Duchess told him on the line. "I need your help."

"You know I stopped assassinating for you long ago."

"Yes, but this isn't about assassinations," she explained. "I want you to send someone after the Pillar in Columbia."

"What's the Pillar doing in Columbia?"

"He's looking for a cure for the plague."

"Why? I was beginning to just enjoy it. Did you know it doesn't affect Wonderlanders?"

"No, I didn't. That's good to hear. But the Queen made her point." Margaret explained how none of them would benefit from the end of the world. Not an argument the Cheshire was fond of.

Who said I wouldn't be happy with the end of the world?

Although he'd never been on good terms with the Queen of Hearts in Wonderland, he'd started to warm up to her and Black Chess a little. After all, he'd been a bit too lonely in this real world.

It was time to choose a side. Black Chess or Inklings.

"Okay," he said. "I will send someone to Columbia."

"You know what kind of someone that is, right? The Executioner will kill anyone who enters his territory."

"Trust me, I know. That's why I can't go there myself. Whatever person I use as a disguise, the Executioner will recognize me. We didn't all stay away from him for nothing in Wonderland. I will send someone."

"Do you mean...?"

"Yes," he said. "Only if I can find them. Because no one's been able to since we left Wonderland."

Chapter 32

Mushroomland, Columbia

"**M**y turn," the Executioner says.

Looking at guards all around us, I wonder what I'm going to do now. I have no way out of this, unless I shoot him and risk being killed one second later.

But why would I shoot him without freeing the children or knowing who cooked the plague?

This is some paradox I'm trapped in.

"So tell me, Alice," the Executioner says. "Do you think you're getting out of here alive today?"

"Hookah Hookah." In my mind, the answer is 'Hell yeah!' I just have no idea how.

"Impressive," the Executioner says. "Even though I know you will die in a few minutes, I still believe you. You know why? Because you definitely believe it. Now ask me."

"Who cooked the plague?" I shoot.

The Executioner laughs. "Hookah Hookah," he says. And I realize that in his mind he just answered, but I am not going to know it, not in a million years. Some silly game.

But wait, he doesn't look like he is telling the truth. What am I supposed to do?

My hand grips my gun. A wide smile forms on the Executioner's face.

That's when I realize how tricky this game is. He deliberately gave me the wrong answer. At least he made sure I'd sense it, so I'd try to shoot him and then have his guards finish me off.

Chapter 33

Never have I been so much on the edge of my seat.

The Executioner's sly grin cuts through me. My hand gripping the gun starts shivering in the nonsensical game played in a nonsensical world. The one thought that is on my brain is: am I still under the mushrooms' influence, unable to make the right decision?

"It's the perfect paradox!" the Pillar compliments the Executioner. "Now, that you're lying—and it shows on your face—she is obliged to pull the trigger and shoot you, but your guards wouldn't let her." He leans forward, looking very amused by the situation. "It's like playing cards with the lion in his den. You winning isn't really going to prevent him from having you for lunch."

An inner voice tells me to pick up the gun and shoot the Pillar instead. I have tolerated many of his crazy actions in the past, but I can't anymore. I should have listened to everyone who warned me of him.

"I applaud you, Executioner." The Pillar stands up, raising his glass. "I mean, shouldn't we toast for this before the girl dies? I totally think we should have this on video."

The Executioner seems puzzled for a moment, shifting his focus from me to the Pillar. Or is it something else that has been going on between them that I am not picking up?

"I didn't think you'd like my trick, Senor Pillardo," the Executioner says. "You really have nothing against killing her?"

"I don't give a Jub Jub about her." The Pillar sips his own drink and let's out a big ah. "Frankly, I brought her here as a gift to you. I mean, all your slave boys are, let's face it, boys. I thought, why not get the Executioner a girl. She's very feisty and can be of pretty good use to you."

I'm tired of gritting my teeth. Who invented it anyways? It doesn't do any good when your anger hurts so much inside.

"But it doesn't make any sense," the Executioner says. "Why would you bring her to me? We both know this isn't true."

I don't know what the Executioner means, but I sense the underlined tension between them.

"Of course it's true." The Pillar asks the guards for one of their hunting knives. "And here is proof." He pulls my hand violently toward him and plasters it on the table, then does the one thing that never crossed my mind. The Pillar raises his knife. "I will cut her two fingers myself. Isn't that how you like your slaves marked? Isn't that what the war beyond Mushroomland is about? All you drug cartels fighting over the kids, so you get the most labor in your business?"

The realization sends surges of lightning into my body. Even though the Pillar is about to mark me, I can't seem to fathom the cruel world, the real world, outside my asylum walls.

"Interesting." The Executioner stands up. "So I suppose you want to know who cooked the plague now in exchange?"

"Now you get it," the Pillar says, tightly gripping my hand. "You said you wanted us to go back to your house, get a meal, and ask me to entertain you. I know you thought we'd shoot jokes and drink like the old days, but this wasn't the kind of entertainment I had cooked for you."

The Executioner laughs, glancing around at his guards. "Senor Pillardo. I don't know what to say. You certainly have entertained me.

I'm surprised I didn't understand at first."

"That's because you're one dumb animal hiding behind an army of poor little kids you think you're enslaving!" I shout at him.

It only makes him laugh more and then address the Pillar. "Shouldn't you cut her fingers first to fulfill the deal?" The Executioner folds his arms and watches.

Again, there is something in the air between those two. Something I'm dying to find out.

"Alice." The Pillar turns to me, lowering the knife to my fingers. "This is going to hurt."

Chapter 34

Somewhere in London

Lewis Carroll had left the church, afraid his followers would lose faith in him seeing his weakness to the migraines.

Walking among the insane people who'd lost their minds, he should have been happy with his work.

But he wasn't.

For two reasons.

The first one was his sudden migraines. Those horrible lightning bolts inside his skull, just like the old days back in Oxford in the 19th century, when he was still a priest and a scholar, long before he wrote the books.

He could remember being part of the Christ Church's Choir, singing and singing for hours, and loving it. But then the migraines began. And he couldn't take the sound of organs or choirs anymore.

He'd run like a madman across the Tom Quad, back to his studio on the roof next to the Tom Tower, kicking and screaming in pain until he fainted all alone on the floor.

One day he woke up from his episode, only to realize he couldn't talk normally anymore. He'd begun to stutter.

And that was when his introverted life began.

Spending hours and hours alone, making up mathematical equations, writing poems, drawing rabbits. The rest was too surreal to remember now.

Still strolling among the mad people of London, he gripped his head as if it was a bomb about to explode. And although he had a plan to follow, he needed to fix his head.

Just like the old days. There was only one substance that could relieve him from the pain. A drug.

But unlike the drug he had someone cook for him for this plague in South America, this drug he needed, or rather cure for his migraine, was only available from the few Wonderlanders left.

He wasn't sure if he should interrupt his plans by searching for the cure for his migraines.

Which brought him to think of the second reason...

Chapter 35

All this time, I thought I was stronger than the Pillar. But I can't free myself from his grip. Seeing his knife sink, it weakens me, thinking I have been fooled.

I can even feel the pain in my fingers before the knife touches them. A string of razor-sharp headaches invade my brain. An image of a school bus flashes before me. Everyone inside is laughing. It's a sunny day, probably spring. I can't see myself in that vision, but I feel butterflies of happiness in my stomach.

The Pillar's knife is on its way down to my fingers.

Then the vision continues. I am trying my best to identify the faces, but I only see Jack. I look harder, but the vision prevents me from looking somehow. However, I recognize the sudden fear on their faces. I turn to look at the driver, hoping it won't be the rabbit, hoping it won't be me like every other hazy memory I have of the incident.

The Pillar's knife touches my fingers. It doesn't cut through yet, but its surface sends shivers to my spine.

The vision continues. My run across the bus seems to take forever. Everyone on it is so scared they don't utter a word. Then I realize they're not looking at the driver. In fact, the bus isn't about to hit anything yet. This part of the vision is way before the accident happened. Everyone is staring at the new passenger getting on the bus. This is who they're scared of.

The Pillar's knife might cut through me. I don't know. Because, for whatever insane reason, I decide to close my eyes. Not against the pain, but to get hold of the memory, trying to recognize the person on the bus everyone is scared of.

The last bit of my vision is even hazier. I look harder at the new passenger, unable to see his face like most of the others. But I am so curious. I squint, press the nerves in my mind somehow. I have to see the passenger who got on the bus a few moments before the accident. And now I see him.

It's Lewis Carroll.

Chapter 36

Somewhere in London

The second reason Lewis wasn't satisfied.

The plague hadn't been fully activated yet. People were only trying to fight each other. That, by far, was nothing to what the plague would make them do in an hour or two.

That... was only the beginning.

And once the plague really kicked in, Lewis had to make his next move.

His last move.

The final touch to his masterpiece.

The reason why he'd planned all of this long ago.

His next move was to find Professor Carter Pillar.

Chapter 37

Mushroomland, Columbia.

"I have an idea." The Pillar pulls the knife back, facing the Executioner. I let out a wheezing breath. "Why would I deny you the pleasure of cutting her fingers yourself?"

My eyes spring open from my vision about Lewis Carroll in my school bus, and then I watch the Pillar hand the knife over to the Executioner, who welcomes the idea immediately.

"Like old days," the Pillar says to the Executioner, who nods like a child, holding the knife and staring at my hand. "Remember those?"

"I was beginning to worry you forgot about the old days." The Executioner smirks. And again, that little secret between those two is driving me crazy. "I'm impressed you still remember vividly."

"Since we're all happy now—the Pillar sips and drinks then tucks in his cigar for the *bazzillionth* time—"I don't see why you won't tell me about who cooked the plague."

The Executioner laughs, struggling to grip my hand. "Why do you really want to know that, Senior?" His men hold me still now. "You don't really want to save the world, do you?"

"I'm aware that your men here will not get affected by the plague," the Pillar says. "All Mushroomlanders are immune to this stuff. But think about it. Who will you sell drugs to if the world dies in the plague?"

The Executioner raises his hand from the knife, as if he had been too stoned to think about this. "Well, you're right," he says. "But this plague isn't about people dying. It's about something much bigger. A higher concept."

"Higher than death? I'm impressed." The Pillar laughs. "But when did we ever care about high concepts, whatever that means? Come on, Executioner, tell me. I promise you I will get back in business and work for you."

This one seems to catch the Executioner's attention the most. "You will do that? Work for me again like in the old days?"

"I swear on all the mushrooms in the world."

The Executioner sighs. "Look, I don't know who cooked the plague. But I know that someone was asking for it about two years ago."

"Go on."

"Someone paid lots and lots of Wonderland money, asking for a specific plague. Under no circumstances am I allowed to tell you what the plague really does to people." This confuses me. There are people in this world even worse than the Executioner? "What I can tell you is that the Wonderlander who'd been asking for the plague had a meeting at the Dodo to pick it up two years ago."

"The Dodo Company?" I ask.

"Not the company. The place." The Executioner talks to the Pillar. "You still remember where that is, right?"

"The Dodo. How could I forget? The most obvious Wonderland location on earth, which no one even considers," the Pillar says. "But I'm curious about this man asking for the plague. Was it Lewis Carroll?"

"That, I can't tell you," the Executioner says, turning back to me, the knife glinting in moonlight. "I think the Dodo information is enough. And now that you're back to working for me, let me enjoy cutting this slave's fingers and marking her as mine."

"Of course." The Pillar bites on his cigar. "Go ahead."

Stranded, I close my eyes, not knowing if I can take the pain. Time seems to slow down. I can hardly breathe, unable to shake myself loose from the soldiers. Waiting for the pain is even worse than the pain itself.

But then I hear some kind of swoosh.

A scream.

Shotguns.

The soldiers let go of me.

When I flip my eyes open, I see the Pillar's cigar stuffed into the Executioner's throat.

Chapter 38

It's really hard to describe what happens from here on.

In the dark, everything happens so fast. Blood spatters everywhere, and the only cause of it is the mysterious Carter Pillar.

First, he stuffed the cigar into the Executioner's throat, snatched the knife from his hands, and stuck it into his back. Then, using the Executioner as a shield, he turned around and started shooting from a machine gun with one hand.

I duck under the table then crawl on all fours to the other side. Whatever is going on, all I think of are the kids. I come up from the other side and run toward them.

With one sneaky look behind me, I see the Pillar is raiding everyone with one machine gun and using the Executioner as a shield. The Pillar shoots like a professional, his face unaffected, cold like stone.

I gather the kids into the Jeep again and get to the wheel, about to drive away.

Then I look back. Should I wait for the Pillar, who is taking the Executioner's men all on his own. Is he going to survive this?

Don't do it, Alice! Just drive away.

For some out-of-this-world reason, I can't. I turn around and drive through the war.

"Pillar," I shout. "I'm coming. Hop in!"

Annoyed, he turns around and starts shooting at the men shooting at the Jeep now. "Who told you to come back?"

"Oh, I'm sorry," I retort. "I should've left you here to die."

The Pillar jumps in, still holding onto the Executioner. The children scream when they see him in the car. The Pillar pulls him to the far side, away from them.

"Where to now?" I shout in the rearview mirror.

"Drive through the mushrooms." The Pillar pulls out a small device and dials a number. "A chopper is coming for us now."

I don't have the guts to ask about the chopper or what just happened. Anything to save us before the machine gun men catch us.

In the mirror, I see the Pillar gently pull a kid's hand and look at the lost fingers. He pats the kid's hand and nods. The kid nods back.

I keep holding on to the wheel, chugging through the muddy ground and mushrooms.

The chopper shows up in the distance. The Executioner's men are still on our tail.

"They'll land right there." He points. "Slow down a bit until they do."

"I can't slow down with those men tailing us."

"Figure it out, Alice," the Pillar roars.

"Alice save us!" the kids chirp.

"Yeah, of course." The Pillar rolls his eyes. "I kill the bad guys, then it's 'Alice save us.'"

Chapter 39

We send the kids safely into the chopper, and the Pillar insists bringing the Executioner along.

Once inside, the chopper takes off, evading the showering bullets from the machine gun men. When I turn to thank the pilot, I am stunned to see it's the Chauffeur.

"You're supposed to be dead."

"I suppose I am supposed to be!" he snickers. "I jumped with my parachute. The Executioner had to think you burned all bridges behind you so he'd trust you."

"So you did all this for him to trust you?" I turn to the Pillar, who is holding the semi-conscious and badly hurt Executioner. "All those games and tricks? But he could've shot me dead on the table."

"I mixed his gun with marshmallow bullets," the Pillar says, his eyes on the Executioner. "Would you like to go back to your people?" he tells him.

The Executioner, now weakened and helpless, still spits and swears at the Pillar in a foreign language. It thaws the kids off. They tuck themselves in the far corner of the chopper.

"You want me to let you go?" The Pillar hands him a parachute. "Sure. You're free to go!"

"Just like that?" I say.

The Executioner puts the parachute on and jumps out of the chopper.

"Like what?" the Pillar says, snaking his way through the kids toward the pilot.

"You let him live?"

"Not at all." The Pillar sits next to the pilot. "I let him fly."

It takes me a second to get it. A smile forms on my face. "The parachute isn't working."

"That's an understatement," the Pillar says. "First, it won't be working. Then, when he pees himself to death in the air, it will start working."

"And?" I am confused.

"Then I push this button." He pulls out a remote control and pushes a button. "It won't work again."

"And now he dies?" I ask. The Executioner is too far down for me to hear if he is screaming or asking for help.

"Not so soon." He presses another button. "Now it works again."

"You're playing games with him?"

"At this precise moment, he is looking at Mushroomland with all the hope in his heart."

"And I suppose you'll push that button and make the parachute not work again?" I am trying to figure this out.

"Nah, it's not me who pushes the button." He summons one of the kids and tells him, "You want to punish the Executioner for what he did?"

The kid nods. I am not comfortable with getting the kids into this, but I need to know what the Pillar has in mind.

"That's it." The Pillar grins after the kid pushes the button.

"Now, the Executioner's parachute won't work anymore," I say.

But then I hear a loud explosion below.

"Boom!" The Pillar jokes with the kids, who laugh from their hearts.

"The Executioner exploded," I say. "Why all this?"

"I could have simply killed him, Alice. But I gave him hope three times and then killed him. Oh, if you only knew how that hurts."

The kids clap their hands from the back. "Senor Pillardo!"

"Now it's him who is cool?" I fold my hands jokingly.

"When you kill a villain, never make it easy for him. I hate when they do that in movies. If I could burn the Executioner in an oven, resurrect him, and burn him all over again, I'd do it." The Pillar pulls out a map and points the pilot where to fly.

"So we're going to this Dodo place?" I stick my head between them. "I hope it's not far."

"Not really." The Pillar adjusts his hat, looking in the mirror. "Peru is just a few miles away."

Chapter 40

London

Possessing an old man's soul inside a pharmacy, the Cheshire watched the news in the TV behind the counter.

The pharmacy's owner had locked his customers in, sheltering them from doomsday outside in the streets of London. The man had a soft spot for old people, so the Cheshire had to possess one, although he hated the slow walk, arching back, and the lost teeth.

"Some loon, that Lewis Carroll." The pharmacist pointed at the BBC's coverage of the Lewis Carroll man attacking another pharmacy, killing everyone violently because they couldn't provided a cure for his migraine.

"Is that the man who spread the hookah plague?" An old woman pointed her cane in the Cheshire's face.

The Cheshire kept his cool. No need to kill humans here while waiting for his phone to ring. He'd made some calls looking for someone to send after the Pillar and was awaiting a response.

"He is the devil," the woman declared. "And he's come for the end of times."

"But he is dressed like a priest," the pharmacist argued.

"They always do, those nasty devils."

"I think he is Lewis Carroll." The Cheshire thought the conversation was fun. "The real Lewis Carroll."

"Who's Lewis Carroll?" the pharmacist said.

"He wrote Alice in Wonderland." The Cheshire was shocked the man didn't know.

"That's the devil's book, too!" The old woman's cane was up to the Cheshire's nose now.

His old-man's nostrils flared. One of the setbacks of possessing people was that he was sometimes limited to their powers. In this case, he could hardly slap this woman if he wanted to.

"Alice in Wonderland," the pharmacist considered. "My kids love that book. I used to love it, too. Never paid attention to the author."

"Why would you?" The Cheshire shook his weary shoulders— they ached. "I never knew of any of the names of the scientists who invented the beautiful medicines that cure us."

"But how is this Lewis Carroll still alive? And why is he looking for this drug so bad?"

"Migraines!" The woman pointed at the TV. "I know how it feels."

"So he is capable of infecting the world with a plague but can't find a cure for his own migraine?"

"The irony of life," the Cheshire commented. Like Carroll, the Cheshire was capable of being anyone, anytime he wanted, except one person, himself, because he never knew who he really was. "He wants it so bad he is killing people now."

In his mind, the Cheshire couldn't understand any of this. Sure, he knew Lewis Carroll in Wonderland, and he'd heard about the man's severe headaches, which at some point contributed to his genius, but how did Carroll turn so violent?

Why did he call himself a Wonderland Monster?

"Look!" the woman said, pointing at the TV again. "People have started killing each other now. It's all around the world."

The Cheshire looked, and it was true. As much as he loved seeing the awful folks of humanity kill one another, he didn't like the expanse of this plague. What started as people going mad had escalated to people turning into murderers all around the world.

Was this the real plague Lewis Carroll was talking about?

The Cheshire checked his phone again, waiting for that reply. He had to find the two Wonderlanders he was looking for. They were the only Wonderlanders capable of entering Mushroomland, along with the Pillar. The Cheshire needed to send them to help the Pillar find the cure.

How ironic, the Cheshire thought, all us Wonderland Monsters hating each other, now trying to collaborate against this Lewis Carroll.

His phone rang. The Cheshire picked up immediately and said, "So, did you find Tweedle Dee and Tweedle Dum yet?"

Chapter 41

Peru

It's the early hours of morning. But instead of landing somewhere in Peru, we're flying over an endless desert.

I don't comment, sharing an anticipated moment with the Pillar and his chauffeur. So are the children in the back. They're fascinated with the desert, which at first confuses me, since there is nothing to see but sand.

Then I realize that the kids have never been out of Mushroomland. This, to them, is their first vacation abroad.

And boy, they love it.

"Where are we really going?" I ask.

"We've arrived," the Pillar says, his eyes scanning the vast earth below. "We're looking for our landing spot."

"Couldn't we just land anywhere? Besides, I thought we were going to Peru."

"There is a bag with a lot of candy in it, kids." The Pillar changes the subject. "Open it up." Oh, he isn't even talking to me. "And there are drinks, too."

I watch the kids happily gorge on the candy, which is shaped like a caterpillar sitting on top of a mushroom.

I finish my candy. It's delicious. I have the children with me, and we're following clues to stop the plague. I think I'm good for now, if only someone would tell me why we're here in the desert, looking for that Dodo location.

All of a sudden, the dessert turns from plain void into an artistic land full of immense drawings. Large artworks that have been etched into the landscape. How? I have no idea.

"They're called geoglyphs," the Pillar says. "Best viewed from above. Actually, you wouldn't grasp what the drawing is about if you stand amidst it."

My candy drops to the floor. My mouth agape. I am stunned.

"This desert plateau stretches more than eighty kilometers long. Geologists prefer to call it the Nazca Lines," the Pillar continues. "Many believe the Nazca Lines were created by the Nazca culture around 500 BC."

"It's that old?" I say while the kids compete for the best view from the top.

"Beautiful, isn't it?" the Pillar says. "Makes you wonder how such an old civilization possessed the craft and knowledge to create something like that."

"What does it mean?"

"That's the centuries-old multi-million dollar question. Just look at the hummingbirds, spiders, monkeys, fish, sharks, orcas, and lizards meticulously crafted on the bed of the earth. No one has any idea what they mean."

"How were they made then?" one of the kids questions.

"The real answer is 'We don't know.'" The Pillar bites on his cigar. I wonder if he's going to stuff this one in someone else's throat. "But common assumption is that the shallow lines were made in the ground by removing the reddish pebbles and uncovering the grayish ground beneath."

When I look closer, I see hundreds of other shapes, most of

animals; birds, fish, llamas, jaguars, monkeys, or human figures. There are also what look like trees and flowers. What strikes me as odd is that most of them look like a geometric design, carefully planned and executed.

"This is incredible," I say. "How did the drawings survive all the time?"

"Again, common knowledge is that it's due to its isolation and the dry and stable climate. There is hardly any wind in this area of Peru," the Pillar says.

"So they have been naturally preserved?"

The kids ask me what this means. I try to explain while listening to the Pillar continue his education. Then one of the kids asks the Pillar, "Did the Nazca have planes?"

"Smart kiddo," the Pillar says. "No, they didn't—or so we think. And although the lines shouldn't necessarily be seen from planes—they can be seen from surrounding foothills, too—it still poses the bigger question..."

I cut in and say, "Why were they created and for whom?

Chapter 42

"It's a complicated question with a complicated answer," the Pillar replies. "In short, we have no idea what the Nazca desert was really meant to be. We just stare at it like primitive monkeys and try to make sense of it. Photographing it, analyzing, and puking theories. Just like Wonderland. It has secrets of its own."

"So why are we here, then?"

"The Executioner told us the meeting took place in the Dodo, right?"

"Yes?" I grimace. "I don't see the connection, other than that it's the same name of the company that manufactured the hookah."

"I am beginning to see the whole picture now. But before I tell you about the connection, I need to make sure you know all about the Dodo," the Pillar says. "Not the one we're looking for but the one in the Alice in Wonderland book."

"What about him? I thought he was a silly lovable character, although I never understood the significance of his appearance."

"The Dodo is Lewis Carroll's alter ego," the Pillar says. "You remember his real name is Charles Lutwidge Dodgson, right?"

I nod. Of course I remember.

"So Lewis used to stutter a lot—I'll get into why he did later. Usually when he tried to say his name was Dodgson, he'd stutter and say Do-Do-Dodgson. Get it?"

"Do-Do," I repeat the words. "The Dodo. That's where it came from?"

"Exactly. Except that this is the kind of stuff historians will tell you," the Pillar says. "I'm not saying he didn't pick the name to reflect on his stuttering. But that wasn't just it."

"There is a bigger picture?"

"There is always a bigger picture if you open your eyes. The dodo is also an extinct bird. And it couldn't fly. There are only records of it, and some claim they see it every now and then, but without concrete evidence."

"Are you saying Lewis was pointing to the bird, too? Why? I don't see a connection."

"Of course you see a connection, an immense one, for that matter." The Pillar points downward, right underneath the chopper.

I look, but it takes me a moment to see it.

Don't get me wrong. It's huge. Immense, like he said. But that's the reason I couldn't grasp what I was seeing at first.

But now I do. There is no question about it. One of Nazca Lines is of a Dodo. And I am staring at it right now.

Chapter 43

The White Queen couldn't believe her eyes.

Standing at the basilica's entrance, the world in front of her had slipped into chaos. It had begun a few hours back after Alice left yesterday. A few tourists began shouting and fighting with one another. But it wasn't much. The police took care of the matter immediately.

And then last night the news of the plague had spread everywhere in Italy. Rome in particular had spiraled into a mad hole of swearing and kicking, something its people were naturally attracted to.

Then the madness escalated at the speed of light.

People everywhere were simply trying to hurt others. You couldn't really make out what the fighting was about, since it was usually caught in its last stages, where fighters uttered no coherent sentences.

It reminded Fabiola of all the wars in the history of the world. Wars that last as long as thirty years, if not more. At some point in, you'd ask either side what they were fighting for, and you could not get an answer. Because none of them remembered what had started this.

This was what the Vatican was turning into. The world was turning into.

Now Fabiola was standing before the basilica, appalled by the fighting taking place in the piazza.

This was a place where people from all over the world came to share common beliefs. This wasn't a place to fight one another, let alone kill one another.

But she had made her decision.

She was allowing the uninfected people to enter the basilica for shelter—it was easy to pick them out; they simply didn't want to hurt anyone else.

Fabiola was about to face a peculiar decision. In a few moments, she was going to close the doors to the basilica and shelter herself with the uninfected. Something she hated to do, because she hated to give up on anyone, even the damned – like her.

Chapter 44

Landing in the middle of the Dodo artwork, I am starting to feel like the Alice in Wonderland in the book all over again.

I mean, most of my journey is about meeting up with the weirdest of the weird characters like in the book. It's like my mind is being opened up to so many ideas and worlds it's driving me crazy. So many times I find myself an observer, yet I can't help but want more.

Curiouser and Curiouser.

"So let's get this straight," I ask the Pillar as we stand alone in the middle of the desert, the chauffeur having taken off again with the kids, "Lewis Carroll knew about this Dodo mark in Peru and decided to mention it in his book?"

"No, that's not it." The Pillar has picked up his cane again, looking around as if searching for an address in this endless maze of desert sands. "The Dodo is Lewis's alter ego, sort of mocking everyone who mocked his stuttering, but at the same time Lewis knew something about the Nazca Lines."

"What is that supposed to mean?"

"Don't you get it?" The Pillar stares back. "Lewis Carroll knew something of the creation of this world. Like his knowledge of

Wonderland, he knew of the past secrets of this real world."

"Let's just hypothetically say that's true." I don't buy any of it. "What does this place have to do with it?"

"I don't know what it is exactly. All I know is that the drug industry in the world was created by the likes of the Executioner, who was once a Wonderland Monster—"

"And I assume you're one of them."

"Yes, Alice. I was a drug lord," he says as if it's about the norm. "And when I was in the business, the Dodo was a major meeting place to pick and hand over certain packages and money. Don't ask me why. What matters is that we're waiting for the man who met with Lewis Carroll and told him how to cook the plague two years ago."

"Okay." I calm myself, trying to cope with too many puzzles. I remind myself that finding the cure is my priority. "So this man who met Lewis here is supposed to just arrive?"

"He usually does when he sees someone waiting here. It's not like you'd find two people arriving here every day."

"I suppose so," I say. "So who is he, the man we we're waiting for?"

"He is a nobody."

"Excuse me?"

"Like I said. We're waiting for nobody." The Pillar points at the vast emptiness.

"Excellent," I resist rolling my eyes this time. "I see nobody on the road."

The Pillar turns to me with a smirk on his face. "Funny, that's exactly what Alice said to the King of Hearts in the book, Alice Through the Looking Glass."

Chapter 45

Surprisingly, I do remember this part in the book, when Alice tells the King of Hearts, 'I see nobody on the road.' It's in the chapter called The Lion and the Unicorn in Alice Through the Looking Glass.

In the book, the King of Hearts replies and says, 'I only wish I had such eyes. To be able to see Nobody! And at the distance too!'

The whole idea of that part is that Lewis Carroll had listed Nobody as a character in the end of the book. Talk about Carrollian madness.

"One of the most underestimated characters of Wonderland." The Pillar points toward a hazy figure arriving on a bicycle in the horizon.

"That's Mr. Nobody, I assume," I say. "The man who we're supposed to meet."

"Here is the catch," the Pillar explains, flashing a wide fake smile at Mr. Nobody. "Those few men who pass valuable information through the desert are all called Nobodies in the drug industry. Why? Because you're not supposed to know their names or see them again. Get it?"

"So you drug people used Lewis Carroll's book references in your sick business."

"On the contrary," the Pillar says. "Nobody and the Executioner lived in Wonderland once."

Before I can comprehend this, Nobody arrives.

He is a bald man, sweaty, too heavy for the meek bicycle he's riding. He grips a large handkerchief, the size of a beach towel, and uses it to mop sweat off his forehead.

Who drives a bicycle in the desert?

"Nobody looks exhausted," I comment.

"That's a double entendre, dear Alice." The Pillar amuses himself. "Do you mean Nobody looks exhausted, or nobody looks exhausted?"

"What's your business here?" Nobody demands in a suspicious tonality.

"The Executioner sent us," the Pillar begins. I assume the word hasn't spread yet about the Executioner's death. "We want to ask you about a certain man you met here two years ago. The one who asked you to cook that hookah plague."

"Ah." Nobody grins. "I remember him. I've also seen the plague's effect in the news. So what's in it for me? Why should I tell you about him?"

"What do you want?" I say. "Money?"

"I have enough of that," Nobody says. "Offer me something I can't resist, or I will tell you nothing."

The Pillar and I exchange brief glances.

"What can a somebody offer a Nobody?" The Pillar rubs his chin.

"If I were you, I'd make it fast," Nobody says. "In case you haven't heard, the plague has wreaked havoc all over the world. At this moment, people are killing each other in the streets. Whole towns are at war with their neighboring towns."

"What?" I haven't had the chance to check the news since I landed in Mushroomland.

"The world is ending much sooner than you think."

Chapter 46

The Queen of Hearts stared down from her balcony at the hordes of citizens wanting to break into the palace and kill her.

If it hadn't been for her guards, she'd have been killed and eaten by those lunatics by now. Those awful human beings. Not only had they humiliated her and every Wonderlander in the Circus, but now they wanted to kill her.

"Margaret!" the Queen yelled. "You ugly Duchess!"

"Yes?"

"What happened with sending someone to find out if the Pillar found a cure?"

"I contacted the Cheshire, who said he'd send someone after him," Margaret said. "But I haven't heard from him since then. Besides, the citizens ransacked many phone towers. It's hard to connect with anyone now."

"So you failed, as always." The Queen stepped up that tall chair so she could shout at Margaret in the face. "I should have your head chopped off," she said. "Who thought Lewis Carroll would just pop up and lash this madness onto us. He's about to destroy the world before I can have my fun torturing everyone."

"I have an idea, My Queen," Margaret said.

"What now? All your ideas are as ugly as you."

"I saw a video of Lewis Carroll looking for the drug for his migraines, which isn't sold in this world, as you know."

"Of course I know it. We used to call it Lullaby. The one pill exclusively made to handle Carroll's hallucinations."

"He's been walking around like a madman, killing pharmacists to stop the headaches. Why not fool him into thinking we have it and bring him here?"

"Here?" The Queen's eyes widened. "You know how much I'm afraid of him."

"He scares us all, but every monster has his weakness. Besides, you can always bring down a man with the power of your endless guards," Margaret said. "They could torture him until he tells us about the cure. Bear in mind that the migraine is killing him. We could give him something that'll worsen it. He will then be weak enough to spill the truth."

"The truth." The Queen waved her hands, the chair underneath her rattling a little. "Everyone wants to know the truth these days. Look, this is your last chance to make things right. Find him and bring him to me – on his knees, if you can."

"Of course, My Queen. I'd say an hour or two, and you will have him in here." Margaret said, having no idea how she could catch a monster like the Lewis Carroll man.

Chapter 47

Nazca Desert, Peru

"**H**ow about we make you a somebody." The Pillar grins back at Nobody.

"You can't keep living your life being a nobody."

Nobody doesn't find it funny.

But seriously, we have nothing to offer this man in this forsaken desert.

"Then I'm sorry." Nobody turns around, about to drive away. "I can't help you."

"Wait," the Pillar says. "I have something for you."

What could the Pillar possibly have?

And in a most devastating moment, the Pillar pulls out a golden key and shows it to Nobody.

It's the key the Hatter took from me.

"Is that what I think it is?" Nobody stares at it with hungry eyes.

I stare at the Pillar as well, only I'm both furious and feeling betrayed.

Did he really fool me last time, playing me all along to get the key?

"It is," the Pillar tells Nobody. "One of the Six Impossible Keys."

"Thank you." Nobody snatches the key from the Pillar's hands while I'm still cemented in place with disappointment. "Now, tell me what you want exactly?"

"What's the cure to the plague?" That's me asking. That's me talking. It helps me put the Pillar's betrayal behind my back for now.

"There is no cure," Nobody says, tucking the key in his pocket.

Furiously, I pull him by his sleeves and roar in his face. "I swear if you don't tell, I will make a somebody out of you, a somebody you will not like at all."

"But what I'm saying is true." He is choking in my hands. I can't help but notice my violent episodes are increasing. And I'm not sure if I like this side of me. "The man who cooked it said so. A plague that can't be cured."

"Who is the man who cooked it?" I tighten my grip.

"They call him the Scientist."

"No name? Just the Scientist?"

"Yes, I swear to God."

"Where can I find this Scientist?"

Nobody is reluctant to say for a moment. He glances toward the Pillar, who's smoking his cigar, fully amused by my anger.

"Tell me!" I shout at Nobody.

His face reddens more, bubbling now, staring pleadingly at the Pillar.

"He's unable to talk, Alice," the Pillar remarks. "You think you're hurting him, but you're actually killing him."

My hands snap away from Nobody. I stare at them as if they aren't mine. What's happening to me?

"The Scientist lives in Brazil," Nobody says, breathing heavily. "He is attending a festival at the moment."

"Having a party while the world is ending," the Pillar says. "Neat."

"I'd go find him now if I was you," the panting Nobody says.

"Suddenly caring about the world?" The Pillar raises an eyebrow.

"You don't understand," Nobody says. "It's not just any festival. It's the famous Brazilian Hookah festival!"

Chapter 48

Nazca Desert, Peru

The moment Nobody tells us where to go next, the Pillar's chopper shows up in the air, ready to pick us up.

"This is when I usually disappear," Nobody says and starts to frantically pedal away.

"You're going to let him leave with the key?" the Pillar says.

It's times like these when I don't know what to do with him exactly. The kids shouting my name in the air distracts me from staring back at the Pillar. I turn and walk in their direction, smiling like a kid myself.

Again, it's funny how little things, like a child's smile, make all the sense in this world of continuous nonsense. Even the Keys to Wonderland don't matter much all of a sudden.

"Hey, Nobody!" the Pillar yells. "You still have my key."

"Who're you talking to?" Nobody twists his head back, mocking the Pillar. "There is nobody on this bicycle."

I actually admire this comeback as the chopper lands before me. The spiraling wind feels refreshing all of a sudden.

"Then I assume nobody is going to fall off the bicycle now." I hear the Pillar suck on his cigar behind me, calling out for the man on a bicycle.

I hear Nobody's bicycle swerve and fall to the ground.

"Ouch!" Nobody wails on the desert floor.

I turn to look.

"I think I heard nobody say ouch." The Pillar strolls casually toward Nobody—which is a boggling sentence, in and of itself.

I suddenly realize the absurdness of a bicycle in the desert. But I am not going to stir my head around that. I've seen madder things in my short life.

The Pillar stands over Nobody and demands the key under the threat of the gun he is pointing at him.

I sense something bad is going to happen. I turn back to the kids and distract them so they don't look.

When Nobody argues he won't give it back, the Pillar shoots his leg. This search for the cure is getting bloodier by the minute.

But it works, and the Pillar gets the key back—my key!

"Don't kill me, please," Nobody begs.

"Only if you tell me the last missing piece of the puzzle," the Pillar says. "Now that we know the plague was cooked by this Scientist, it's time to tell us who ordered it in the first place."

"I thought you were sure it was Lewis Carroll," I interfere from the distance. "Isn't he the Wonderland Monster who's behind this?" Of course, I still have my doubts about Lewis being a monster, but I haven't been sure of anything for a while.

"Who is it?" The Pillar lowers his gun toward Nobody, neglecting me.

"Carolus Ludovicus!" Nobody finally speaks.

This is the moment a whirlwind sweeps through the desert, almost knocking me off the earth.

When it slows down, I see the Pillar is still pointing his gun. Even from this far, I can see the worried look on his face.

Carolus Ludovicus?

The name sounds villainous. Another drug lord from around here? Then what about this Lewis Carroll walking the streets of London?

"You understand now when I told you the plague is incurable?" Nobody tells the Pillar.

The Pillar says nothing, turns around, shoots the man dead without looking, and walks toward me.

The look on his face is tense.

"You didn't have to shoot him." I talk to him as he gets on the chopper. "I know he was a bad man, but I'm fed up with all this killing."

"Did I shoot someone?" The Pillar fakes an innocent face. The children laugh.

"Yes." I get in. "You shot Nobody."

The children laugh again, and now I get the joke.

"Exactly." The Pillar signals for his chauffeur to take off. "I shot nobody."

Chapter 49

Radcliffe Asylum, Oxford

Tom Truckle, protected by the asylum's guards, welcomed his twin son and daughter and pulled them inside immediately.

"Issue Plan-X now," he ordered his guards, hugging his teenagers.

But Todd and Tania weren't fond of their father. They never had been. Tom knew they'd only accepted his call to shelter themselves from the apocalypse outside.

Tom showed them to the underground ward and tucked them safely in the best cell possible.

"It's not clean," Tania protested.

"Horrible," Todd followed. "Just like you, Dad."

"How about a little patience?" Tom argued. "Once all is set, I'll get Waltraud or Ogier to clean it for you."

"Waltraud?" Tania raised her thick eyebrows.

"Ogier?" That was Tom.

Both of them laughed hysterically. Although boy and girl, sometimes when they laughed like this, he couldn't tell who was who for a moment. All Tom knew was that his kids tended to be a little evil from time to time.

"Enough with that," he said. "Look, why don't you two play with that lovely Flamingo in there?"

Todd and Tania marched toward it, not lovingly but more like they were disgusted by it.

"Okay." Tom pulled them back, realizing he cared for the Flamingo more than anything. "Just wait here. I know who can show you discipline around here. Waltraud!"

But Waltraud didn't reply.

Tom called for her again.

And again.

Finally, one of the guards told him Waltraud had left the asylum.

"Why?" Tom questioned. "She loves it in here. She adores the Mush Room."

"But she loves the world outside better now," the guard said. "She took her baseball bat with her and told us she wouldn't miss all those fights outside."

Before Tom could comment, his twins, Todd and Tania, summoned him again, complaining about something else in the cell. No matter how hard he tried to please them he couldn't, but he had to go grant them one more wish.

"Yes, Tweedles," he said. "I'm coming over."

Their mother used to call them Tweedledum and Tweedledee when they were younger.

Chapter 50

Hookah Festival, Brazil

The festival isn't going to start until the sun goes down. We have no choice but to wait until then. Which is a big risk. Our journey has taken about two days, and I remember Carolus saying it would only be three days before the plague took its course to end the world.

But even so, I spend the time with the kids, showing them around and buying them clothes and candy. The Pillar provides the money for the clothes, but that doesn't mean I want to talk to him.

Every time I remind myself that he was the real Mad Hatter, playing me around to get the key, I can't bring myself to look him in his face. I truly regret going back for him in Columbia. I should have left him to get eaten by the Executioner's men.

I am aware I still need him for this mission, so I won't push it. But after this ends, the Pillar and I will part ways. I don't care what his story is. It's a sensitive issue when someone betrays me.

I will even talk again to Fabiola about the Inklings. We should find a way to pay the Pillar back—although I don't see how it's possible. Maybe that's why he bought it for me; to use it to manipulate me, make me feel in debt, so I would never stand up to him.

Deep inside, I admit I feel he is a much better man than he seems to be. I mean he saved me from the Executioner. But every time I tell myself that, he turns the table on me in a blink of an eye.

My predicament is truly weakening me. I mean, even Lewis Carroll is some kind of a monster now. How am I going to live with that? Am I really supposed to not trust anyone but myself? Are these the rules of the game?

The kids try their clothes on. They seem to be fond of brightly colored dresses. I don't blame them. They lived in a dim mushroom world for so long.

I make sure everyone gets what he wants, not knowing what I am going to do with them. I can't take them back to the asylum. That would be like transporting them from one hell to another.

But I'll figure it out.

Right now I have to send them back to the chopper, so the Pillar and I can get ready for the hookah festival that night.

Chapter 51

Haha Street, Department of Insanity, London

Inspector Sherlock Dormouse was about to order a lockdown on the department when the Lewis Carroll man walked in.

Each and every one of the police officers stopped with their mouths open wide, staring at him. For one, he was scary as hell. And two, it made no sense for a criminal to walk into the department on his own.

Inspector Dormouse didn't feel the need to fall asleep now. How could he with that monster walking in his office? He watched the lankly man stroll through, not saying a word. He seemed to be looking for something.

The man was tense, gripping his head and sweating like he had an intolerable headache. He was sweating and drooling. He was in dire pain.

But he kept on walking, stopping next to the room where they locked criminals in—well, they hadn't used it for some time because they never caught anyone.

The Lewis Carroll man stood in front of the barred cell and turned to face the sweating Inspector.

"Keys," he demanded.

"Keys?" Inspector Dormouse raised his eyebrows.

"Keys."

"Keys?" the rest of the officers replied, eyes wide open with surprise.

"*Keysss*," the monster grunted.

"Keys! How many times does he have to ask for the keys?" Inspector Dormouse yelled at the officers.

One of them threw the cell's keys on the Inspector's desk. Sherlock Dormouse wished he was asleep now, so he wouldn't have to hand them himself to the Lewis Carroll maniac.

Slowly, he reached for them then started tiptoeing his way toward the monster. "There is no need to lock us inside the cell," the Inspector managed to say, his lips shivering and his belly flipping like jelly. "We can just leave and you can enjoy the department all alone. Right, officers?"

All the officers nodded in silence.

The Lewis Carroll man snatched the keys from the Inspector and opened the cell with it.

Then he did something unexplainable.

He entered the cell, locked himself inside, and gave the keys back to the Inspector.

Chapter 52

Hookah Festival, Brazil

It's hard to fully comprehend what's going on in the Hookah Festival, not with all this spiraling smoke around us.

"I love it!" The Pillar raises both arms in the air, welcoming the show.

"Of course you love it." I roll my eyes. "All the hookahs you can smoke for a lifetime."

"You have no idea what you're talking about, Alice. This is where imagination runs wild," the Pillar says as we snake through the endless crowd. He inhales every flavor we come across as if it's the battery of his soul. "Look at all this haze."

"There is nothing to look at. I can barely see anything."

"And that's the point exactly."

"The point is not to see what's ahead of me?"

"The point is to see enough to get you going, and then keep the rest of it a mystery."

"And why would I want whatever is in front of me to be a mystery?"

"Oh my, Alice. Can't you see this festival is a metaphor for life? What good is it if you know what tomorrow holds for you? One hookah puff at a time, young girl."

Instead of arguing, or actually considering his logic, I see him greeting all fellow hookah's he passes by. At least I can see that far.

"Banana-flavored hookah!" The Pillar celebrates. "You have to try this one, Alice."

"No, thanks. I've had my share of dizziness already." Would I risk experiencing the mushrooms' effect again?

"How about Blueberry?" he offices.

"Aren't we supposed to find the Scientist?"

"But of course," he burps. "Mr Scientist!" Spiral bubbles form out of his mouth when he speaks. "Not here."

I don't know if it's funny or horrible when I see him act like a kid. Thank God I told the Columbian kids to wait in the chopper, or this would have turned into a kindergarten.

"How about this one?" He hands me a hookah that writes random words in the air when you blow out the smoke. How this is possible, I have no idea.

Who r u? The Pillar writes in the air, just like a 1951 Disney movie.

I have to admit. I am tempted to try it. But I realize I am just wasting time while I have a lot of questions.

"Pillar." I pull him by his sleeve. "I had a vision where I saw Lewis Carroll in the bus accident."

This stops him from having fun.

He faces me with a keen look in his eyes, but says nothing.

"Does that look mean you knew about this?"

"Not knew, but the assumption had crossed my mind," the Pillar says. "Bear in mind I have no idea what happened on the bus. I only found you after that, when I got into the asylum."

"So why did you assume Lewis Carroll was on the bus?" I say. "My brain is about to explode. It's all so confusing. Why is Lewis a Wonderland Monster?"

"Because it's not exactly Lewis who you saw on the bus. Nor is he the man who plagued the world with his hookahs."

"Then who is that man looking so much like Lewis?"

"Didn't you hear nobody say his name? Carolus Ludovicus."

"I'm not following. Who is Carolus Ludovicus?"

"The hardest Wonderland Monster to kill," the Pillar says. "Because he is also Lewis Carroll."

Now my head spins even more.

Chapter 53

Hookah Festival, Brazil

We walk among the festive Brazilian crowd as the Pillar tries to explain things to me.

"You remember when I told you Lewis Carroll's real name?" he asks me.

"Of course I do. This is the second time you've asked me this. Charles Lutwidge Dodgson."

"Charles was looking for a pen name to use for his book, Alice in Wonderland," the Pillar begins. "Let's skip why he needed a pen name for the book for now. What matters is that he spent weeks looking for a special name. One of his ideas was to try to translate his real name to Latin. Charles in Latin is Carolus."

"I've never heard this before."

"Because people are usually obsessed with books, not their authors." The Pillar walks next to me in the haze.

"And Lutwidge is Ludovicus?"

"Now you get it," the Pillar says. Fireworks play all around us. "But then you realize how villainous the name sounds. Interesting but villainous. So he decided to play with it a little. First move was to try Ludovicus Carolus.

"And then?"

"With a little word play, it became Louis Carol, and finally Lewis Carroll."

"I understand. But it doesn't explain him becoming a Wonderland Monster, or is he?"

"Let's put it this way. Lewis took drugs like any other Victorian authors in a time when it was a common and legal practice. And like most artists, they're usually stimulated by pain or euphoric substances. Don't make count the endless names in history who'd prove my theory."

"I don't agree with you, but continue anyway."

"Lewis' headaches were the main reason for his addiction. A drug, or rather a cure, called Lullaby, a Wonderlastic invention," the Pillar says. "The drug helped with his migraines, which he had explained as splitting his head in two. There is a famous scribbled drawing of him with a split brain found in his diaries."

"An image he drew himself?"

"Yes. Lewis used to beat the migraines with art, poetry and masterpieces, until he desperately needed Lullaby."

"Which I assume the Executioner and his people provided back in Wonderland."

"Exactly, and the tricky part is that Lewis still lived in Oxford at the time. He had found a way to move between the two worlds and get his fix."

"Still, this doesn't explain..."

"Just bear with me. So the drug worked for a while, until the Queen of Heart found out about Carroll's need. Since this was at the peak of conflicts in Wonderland, the Queen ruling with an iron fist and Carroll trying to create the Inklings to oppose her, she made sure the drug disappeared from the face of Wonderland."

"And then Lewis had continuous headaches without a cure."

"The headaches intensified so much he began to draw many

of those split images of himself," the Pillar says. "Sir John Tenniel, Carroll's painter and good friend, noticed this and warned him of the consequences. But Carroll just loved his art and wouldn't stop, even with his killer migraines. Tens of times, they found find him lying comatose on the floor in his studio. And when he woke up, he didn't remember where he was and what he had done."

"I don't like where this is going."

"I know. Sadly, it's the truth. Carroll was turning into Carolus Ludovicus when he passed out."

"What? Like a case of Dr. Jekyll & Mr. Hyde? Lewis had some kind of a split personality? This explains why the man in London is the real Lewis Carroll," I say. "Poor Lewis. He just needs help. Someone to wake him up from this dark alter ego."

The Pillar stops to face me. I've known him long enough to know this is the moment when he drops a bomb on me.

"It would have been easier if all that happened to him was discovering he just had a monster inside him," the Pillar says. "One day, Lewis woke up from his episode and saw someone sitting opposite him at the table."

"Someone?"

"Someone who looked like him."

I don't say anything. I only tilt my head in disbelief.

"Lewis Carroll was staring at Carolus Ludovicus in the flesh," the Pillar says as the fireworks light the sky in red above us. "His other and darker self, manifested as a separate and real being. A Wonderland Monster."

Chapter 54

Haha Street, Department of Insanity

Inspector Dormouse looked back and forth between his officers and the Lewis Carroll man. "Well, that's the first time we've ever caught a criminal in this department." He chuckled. "Unless you count last week's rabbit a criminal, which I didn't end up catching anyway."

The Lewis Carroll man said nothing. It made everyone worry. Those kind of Wonderland Monsters were never really constrained by bars. Something was really wrong.

"My name isn't Lewis Carroll," the monster finally spoke, gritting his teeth against the headache. "Carolus Ludovicus."

"Okay?" Inspector Mouse said.

"Those bars mean nothing to me. I can break through anytime I want," Carolus said. "But I am giving you the pleasure of catching me, under one condition."

"And what could that be?" Inspector Dormouse asked.

"Tell the Queen of England I want to meet her. I know how to stop the plague. But I'll only do it if she gives me the cure for my headaches in exchange."

Chapter 55

Hookah Festival, Brazil

I once heard this song that I liked so much. It's called: *The Show Must Go On* by Freddy Mercury.

The reason why it comes to mind while I snake my way through the endless smoke of the hookah festival is that it seems to describe what I am feeling exactly.

Think about it. In less than 48 hours, I've realized the Pillar betrayed me, I've met with one of the lowest scumbags on earth, the Executioner, and I've just realized the pain Lewis Carroll went through.

I mean, who can live with his own split persona manifesting into a real enemy? An enemy who is in many ways you.

The darker you.

The you with all those thoughts you could never share with anyone.

The you with all those ideas you never knew you had buried in a grave in the back of your mind.

The you... who isn't really you.

Making sure I don't let the Pillar out of sight, my mind is as foggy as the hookah smoke surrounding us. It seems to me, and I'm not the best candidate to say this, that the Cheshire was right. And he always will be. We're all mad here.

The one thing I'd add to his famous phrase would be: *So there is no need to point fingers. The world is a marshmallow bubble of mess. Enjoy it while you can.*

A few minutes ago I asked the Pillar if he knows why Carolus was on the bus. The Pillar said he knew nothing of the bus or what happened in it. He also said that whatever I had imagined was likely hallucinations from the mushrooms. I don't know what to believe.

"Alice!" The Pillar's voice pulls me back into the real world. "Have you seen this?" He shows me a hookah with an elephant's hose. "Nutty-tutty weird, right?"

I fake a smile. "I'm going to ask you again. How will we get to that Scientist?"

"Scientisto, if I may correct you," the Pillar says. "I asked around, and that's what they really call him."

"They don't know his real name?"

"Nor does he have an address. But they say he looks like the mad uncle from Back to the Future."

"I don't know what that is."

"A fun movie from the eighties. You weren't born yet. Don't bother."

"So that's all?"

"Not exactly," The Pillar raises his voice against the fireworks and hailing crowd. Some special event is about to take place. "The Scientisto is like a god here. Common belief is that he will send his men to meet with him if he senses you're special."

"And how are we supposed to do that?"

"I was told the next event is a good opportunity."

"This one?" I point at the crowd in the distance. They're standing next to a tall wall, and it seems the smoke lessens as I walk closer.

"I believe so."

"How can we show him we're special in that event? What is it called?"

"How? I have no idea. What is it called? Oh, I know that, and I love it."

"I'm listening."

"It's something Lewis would have loved a lot," the Pillar says, snaking through the crowd. "It's called Phantasmagoria."

Chapter 56

Settling among the others in the Phantasmagoria event, I see a big truck spurting out big chunks of fire in the air. The flames are thick and light up the night, high enough not to hurt anyone. However, the angle makes our shadows visible on the enormous wall we're looking at.

I am still not sure what this event or game is.

"Phantasmagoria is one of Lewis's craziest poems," the Pillar says, sounding festive like everyone else. "No one really knows what it means, but it's also the name of a form of theatre in France in the 18th century, and late in England in the 19th century. A very interesting and well known one actually."

"Theatre? The name sounds like something scary."

"It is, actually. The Phantasmagoria theatre used a modified magic lantern to project frightening images onto the walls."

"Frightening as in...?"

"Skeletons, ghosts, and so forth. It happens all the time. Haven't you ever been to the beach and had the camp fire reflect your shadow in scary forms?"

"I haven't been to the beach," I say. "But I get the idea."

"Some artists used semi-transparent screens, frequently using rear projection later," the Pillar says. "The projector was mobile, allowing the images on the wall to change size on the screen, which, in our current case, will be the wall in front of us."

Glad to know what the wall is for. Also, I know the fire behind us is meant to cast our shadows on the wall now.

"Of course, there are many variations of the practice," the Pillar says. "Some were able to cast quick switching images to tell a short story, to show a girl run from a ghost. It was much loved in its time."

"And we're going to play it here now, with the fire reflecting our shadows?"

"Not just the fire, the hookahs' smoke too. You can either use the smoke to manipulate the image or to add another layer. Be creative."

We start to stand in line next to one another, facing the wall. I'm starting to sweat heavily. The area is getting hotter because of the fire, never mind the Brazilian humidity."

But I am rather enjoying this. The reflections on the walls are funny. People bend their bodies, stretch their arms, and sometimes use an external element to manipulate the shapes on the wall. There is a man whose reflection is a big duck. Another makes his body look like a boat. It's brilliant. I think the kids would have enjoyed this.

The Pillar borrows a few balloons from others and manipulates his image into a caterpillar sitting atop a mushroom. People go crazy when they see that. They love it.

"Now that's something special." The Pillar winks at me.

"I wish the caterpillar was real," a little girl comments. "I love him."

"He loves you too, darling." The Pillar smiles.

"How do you know?" The girl pouts. "You're not the caterpillar."

I burst out laughing. The Pillar's cheeks redden.

We keep on watching others. Three men manipulate the image into three dogs eating peanuts. I tilt my head back to the Pillar for explanation.

"They all know the Queen of England eats their precious nuts here," he says. "None are left for the masses, so they have to make fun of her."

"Uh-huh. So I am still lost at that something special idea. I see most people are doing incredible things. What could be more special than that?"

"I have no idea," the Pillar says. "We have to think of something that would attract a man who just cooked a plague to kill everyone on the other side of the world."

I have no idea what that could be. It occurs to me that I don't know anything about that Scientisto. "I wonder if the Scientist is also a Wonderlander."

"A very plausible assumption." The Pillar looks impressed. "But I don't know of a scientist in Wonderland."

"Let's just say he is." I have a dangerous idea in my mind.

"Okay. Let's just say that. So what? Are you going to manipulate your image into writing Wonderland on the wall?"

"No," I say. "In fact, I don't need to manipulate anything."

The Pillar stops his moves and stares at me. It's that look again in his eyes when he admires my actions. "You have my undivided attention and heart-pounding anticipation."

I smile and slip my hands into the Pillar's pocket, pulling out the key.

Chapter 57

"That's a very smart idea," the Pillar says.

"I know. I don't need you to tell me that." I hold up the key and adjust my angle so it reflects on the wall.

Of course, it doesn't reflect immediately. The key is too small, and the fire is a bit far from where I stand. I run through the crowd, the Pillar following me, until I find the spot with the fire nearest to the wall.

Not just that. I spend some considerable time finding the right spot where the key's reflection is big enough to be noticed. It doesn't really get that big, but it's enough for the Scientist's attention—that's if my assumption is right.

"Seems like it wasn't a great idea after all." The Pillar pouts, looking around for the Scientist's men.

But my stubborn genes tell me it should work. Even if the Scientist isn't a Wonderlander, the key should attract someone's attention. This isn't possible.

"I am afraid to ask, but I need my key back." The Pillar shrugs.

"You know it's not your key," I say, giving it back to him. "But I don't want it. At least not now. And for the record, I don't ever want to talk to you again after we save the world this time."

"Are you so sure you're going to save the world this time?" He tucks the key in his jacket pocket and rubs off some smoke.

It's questions like these that make me doubt myself.

Of course I am not sure I'm going to save the world this time. And it scares me to even think about it.

I think about those children again. The world can't end on their first day of freedom. They still have so much to enjoy and learn in life, or has the Executioner already sentenced them to death in his grip?

I realize I would have preferred to choke him myself instead of listening to the explosion.

And there is something else I realize now. That Fabiola was right. If you stare into the eyes of darkness, you will always get stained.

"I'm thinking of pull off my pants and let out gas into the smoke the Scientist will definitely notice me." The Pillar rubs his chin. "I know it's lame, but so were many of Carroll's jokes."

Lewis!

That's the answer to how to get the Scientist's attention. The Pillar's key may be valuable to many Wonderlanders, but definitely not like the one I have in my pocket.

Sorry, Lewis, I will break our promise. But I have to give it a shot.

I raise the key in the air and stand in that same spot again. Carroll's key reflects in a shimmering hue over the wall.

"You have another key?" The Pillar can't take his eyes of it. "Who's the liar now?"

I dismiss his comments, still staring at the wall.

Then it happens. Not the way I expected, but close. A loud, deafening horn blares in the festival.

Chapter 58

Queen's garden, Buckingham Palace, London

"**W**elcome back, Carolus." The Queen of Hearts stood in the middle of the rain, two of her guards holding her umbrella for her. "It's time we solve this matter."

"What matter?" Carolus spat rain in her face.

"Your headaches," she said. "You know without me stopping the Executioner from giving Lewis his medication, you would have never been created in the first place."

Carolus grunts, trying to step closer, but he was chained in heavy steel, and guarded carefully. Finally Margaret did her job right, the Queen thought.

"I'm like your god by the way." The Queen smirked. "I could have given Carroll his medication anytime, and you'd have disappeared. You have any idea how unreal you are? You're neither Carroll nor Carolus. You're just a figment of his imagination that manifested somehow."

"Don't provoke me," Carolus growled and broke free from the chains. The Queen's guards stepped away immediately.

"Don't threaten me!" The short Queen's head ached, craning it up to him.

"What are you going to do? Cut my head off?" He laughed, still spitting rain at her.

"I don't need to." She grinned.

Instantly, Carolus's migraine returned. He fell to his knees, gripping his skull.

"See?" the Queen chirped. "My men fooled you into thinking the pills they gave you were Lullaby when they only worsened your headache."

"Stop it, please!"

"You should have asked for your cure back in Columbia instead of cooking up a plague," she said. "But because you're just a figment of someone's imagination, you couldn't think straight. All you thought of was ending the world for no apparent reason, just because you were in pain."

"It's not just that..."

"Stop it!" She kicked him in the foot. "Stay on your knees when I am talking to you. And listen to what I have to say."

Carolus said nothing. All he could do was grip his head before it exploded.

"I will have the Executioner supply you with endless amounts of Lullaby." She pointed her finger at him. "Under one condition."

"I'll do anything," the vicious monster said pleadingly.

"If you tell me how to stop the plague."

"I can't," he stuttered. "The plague is unstoppable. I just told you I knew because I needed my Lullaby pill!"

Chapter 59

Hookah Festival, Brazil

The blaring horn puts the festival to a halt.

Not only that, but most of the crowd around us scurry away like rats. The Pillar and I are left alone inside a haze of smoke and fire.

Neither of us say anything for a long time. Anticipation? Fear? I have no idea. But I can hear the footfalls of dozens approaching us from behind the smoke.

"It occurs to me that we've not been told if getting the Scientist's attention could lead to our deaths," the Pillars says, trying to see through the fog of hookah smoke.

It's hard for me to utter any words now. I realize what might be in danger is not the Pillar or me but Lewis's key.

Staring at it, I don't know where to hide it. Was it stupid of me to use it? Lewis was clear about not losing it. An insane idea hits me. What if I swallow it? I've seen them do that in movies.

But I am not going to swallow it. No way. I tuck it inside my shoe, wishing it to be a good idea.

The footfalls are nearing now. Everyone else in this festival has disappeared.

"Anything you want to say before you die?" the Pillar tells me.

"Not to you," I counter back. 'I hate you' is what my eyes say. Even in this haze. Then I realize I'm curious about something. "Maybe it's you who wants to tell me something before you die. The Executioner. What was going on between you two?"

Unexpectedly, the Pillar's face changes. It dims in such an unhealthy way. What happened between you and the Executioner, Professor Pillar?

His dimming face doesn't last long, though. His eyes widen as our pursuers show up from behind the haze of smoke.

I am surprised I recognize them. But I'm not sure how they fit into all of this.

"If I had a mushroom for every time I run into one of you," The Pillar pouts, staring at the Reds.

As usual, they are dressed in their numbered, red cloaks, their faces hidden underneath them.

"You want to meet up with the Scientist?" one of them says, his voice deep and hollow, as if from another world.

"Yes." I stand up straight.

"You will have to drink this before we bring you to him!"

The Pillar looks away from the drink. "I'm not drinking that."

"What is it?" I ask.

"Hmm." He hesitates.

"It's the drink he made you drink in the rabbit hole in the Garden of Cosmic Speculation," one of the Reds explains.

I sneer at the Pillar. He starts whistling, staring up as if admiring the night stars.

Then I realize I have to ask something, "And how do you, Red, know about that?"

"You don't seem to realize who we are, Alice," their leader says, his voice implying mockery. "Just drink this, or you will not see the Scientist."

I have no choice but to accept. What harm will that do? I am used to seeing things bigger in scale. It's not that bad actually.

But as I bring myself to drink it, the Red's sentence rings in my head. *You don't seem to realize who we are, Alice.*

Does that mean they're working for the Pillar? Does that mean I have been fooled again?

Chapter 60

Somewhere in Alice's mind.

The drink, unlike last time, puts me to sleep.

It's a different kind of sleep because I know I am sleeping. I know I am dreaming. And I don't like where my dreams have sent me.

I dream I am back in the Radcliffe Lunatic Asylum. I dream I am back on that couch in that dark psychiatry room.

I hate this room.

"So how deep have you gone into the rabbit hole, Alice?" the doctor, hiding behind his smoke and darkness, tells me.

"I want to wake up!"

"You're not dreaming, Alice. This is your reality, like I've told a thousand times."

"No, you're a figment of my imagination. Some kind of a sick joke."

"Alice. Alice. Alice." The doctor puffs his pipe. "Haven't we talked about this before? The rabbit hole. Remember when I told you I would let you delve deeper into your madness, until you couldn't take the nonsense anymore? That's the moment when you'll realize you're mad."

"I don't believe you. I'm not mad. I am saving the world."

The doctor says nothing, trying to suppress a laugh, I think.

"Have you ever considered that you're the mad one?" I say. "Maybe this is your rabbit hole, and you think you're some psychiatrist in an asylum."

"It seems that you haven't had enough of the rabbit hole yet." He sighs. "I think we're done for today."

"I think so, too," I retort. "Because I'd really like to wake up to go complete my mission."

"And where is it this time?"

"Brazil."

"And you're saving the world from what?"

"A plague."

"What kind of plague?"

This is when I hesitate. I don't even know what kind of plague this is. All I know is that it has driven people so crazy they're killing each other all around the world.

In my moment of embarrassment and silence, I wonder what this plague really does to people. The Executioner said it's something unimaginable. That's why it has no cure. But really, what drives people mad enough to start killing each other all around the world?

"I take it that you don't know what kind of plague." There is victory all over the doctor's voice. "I'll have the wardens take you back, but I'm afraid you need a higher dose of your medicine this time."

"Medicine?" I know in this dream I am always given medicine, but I haven't paid attention to it.

"Your medicine, Alice." He sounds impatient or disappointed. I can't really tell. "The pill I've been giving you for two years now. It's called Lullaby, if you remember."

Chapter 61

Brazil

In spite of all the confusion, the mixed emotions, the drink's effect is hilarious. I wake up laughing like I haven't for some time. It's the kind of laughing that cramps the stomach and makes you wiggle your feet or hands. And the funniest part of it is that I don't know why.

Could it be because everything around me looks so big?

This room I am in is definitely hot and humid, but its doors are the size of a fortress. The windows are, too, and it takes me a while to realize they are in fact windows. And this desert of velvet I'm walking on is nothing but the sheets of normal-sized bed.

I laugh harder when I see the Pillar the same size as me. He looks really annoyed, and it makes me happy.

"See? This is the same way I felt when you drugged me in the rabbit hole, pretending you were the Mad Hatter," I say.

The Pillar is too annoyed to even answer me. He keeps shouting the Scientist's name.

"But wait a minute," I say. "This means the Reds aren't working for you?"

"The Reds are hired mercenaries, Alice. I hired them last week, like others hire them all the time," the Pillar says. "They once worked for the Queen of Hearts, and some of them still do, but those don't call themselves Reds anymore."

"Are you saying the Scientist has hired them now?"

"Looks like it. Where are you, Scientisto!" he shouts.

"I'm here," a deafening sound answers. "I had to use the Alice Syndrome on you so as to keep my identity secret."

It's true. All we see is someone huge talking to us. It's hard to tell who he is. Still, his loud voice, in proportion with his size, is annoying.

"So let's cut this short," the Pillar raises his voice, in case the Scientist can't hear us clearly. "We know Carolus asked you to cook this plague for him. We need you to cook us the cure."

I am curious about how this Alice Syndrome works. This is not exactly like the one I experienced in the rabbit hole. I mean, here we're really small. And what boggles my mind is that I know that we're not small. It's just the effect of the drink.

It's tremendously uncomfortable.

"There is no cure to the plague," the Scientist says.

"Come on," I shout. "What kind of virus has no cure? There must be one."

"This plague is like no other. It's not a virus."

"Why does everyone tell us that?" the Pillar says. "You make it sound as if it's not a chemical plague. Is it some kind of magic?"

"Worse."

"Tell us, Scientisto," I say. "Please."

"I'll pay double whatever Carolus paid you," the Pillar offers.

"All the money in the world can't cure the truth."

"The truth?" the Pillar and I ask in unison.

"Yes. Carolus wanted a plague that wasn't just incurable, but also ironic," the Scientist says. "Like most Wonderlanders who were in the Circus, he wanted to laugh at the world. He wanted to give them a poison of their own."

"I'm not quite following." The Pillar suppresses a thin smile on his lips. Of course he's amused about the idea. He just wants the Scientist to spell it out for him.

"The Hookah of Hearts plague makes people tell the truth."

Chapter 62

Queen's garden, Buckingham Palace, London

Margaret watched the Queen of Hearts lay on her stomach on the floor, kicking her hands and feet. The Queen couldn't stop laughing so hard Margaret and the guards felt embarrassed for her. They also didn't quite understand what Carolus said that was so laughable.

"You infected the world with telling the truth no matter what?" Tears of joy sprang out of her eyes. "Brilliant. Bloody Brilliant!"

The only one who shared her point of view was Carolus. Tied in a special execution chair, and still aching with migraines, he let out a few chuckles. He looked satisfied someone appreciated the idea, but he certainly didn't get a kick out of it like the Queen.

Hiccupping, the Queen walked up, her face red like a pumped tomato. She adjusted her dress, trying to suck the laughs in around her guards. But it was only seconds before she started again.

"May I ask why this is supposed to be so funny, My Queen?" Margaret asked.

"Don't you get it?" the Queen said. "Imagine a father returns home to his wife and children. He shouts 'Honey, I'm home,' And his wife goes like, 'Why did you come back? I prayed to the Lord that you'd get hit by a train on the way.' And the husband goes like, 'Like I haven't prayed the same thing for you all of those years.' Then their child walks into the room and says, 'Papa, you're fat. And bald. My friends laugh at you. And mama, your cooking sucks.' And from then on imagine the trail of honesty escalating until someone physically hurts the other."

Margaret didn't know whether to laugh or not, but she certainly hadn't grasped the wickedness of the plague at first. Come to think of it, most of us passed the days by lying to each other.

"Now imagine this happening at work," the Queen said. "Imagine what kind of atrocities the employees would tell their boss. And so on and so on."

Then why haven't I felt the need to swear at you, obnoxious queen, all day? Margaret fidgeted at the thought.

"Imagine you had to tell the truth, Margaret, huh? You'd be spitting in my face now and telling how much you despise me." The Queen stepped forward to face her assistant. "And what would that lead to? I'd order your head chopped off. But then you'd call the Cheshire before you died and order him to assassinate me. And then I'd give Carolus his Lullaby pill and order him to eat the Cheshire for lunch. Do you now grasp the magnitude of the plague?"

"I guess I do." Margaret fiddled with the blood-diamond ring on her finger. "Carolus managed to plague the world with the one thing people claim they demand the most. Transparency, honesty, and truth."

"The only things they are truly—pun intended—not capable of. It's brilliant!"

Chapter 63

Brazil

It takes me a while to digest the truth about the truth about the *truth*.

And as the drink's effect starts to wear off and I start to return to my normal size again, it's hard to imagine how Carolus came up with the idea. It's even hard to imagine what a plague of truth would do to this world.

In my mind, I try to think of the asylum as my small rat lab for a truth experiment. What would happen if I told Waltraud and Ogier how I felt about them? I'd end up in perpetual shock therapy until I fried like grilled chicken.

And then what if Waltraud told Dr. Tom Truckle how she thought he was the maddest of all and that he belonged in a cell like every other mushroomer?

And what if Tom told himself he was addicted to his pills? He'd probably admit himself to the asylum.

But what if every Mushroomer in the asylum told the truth? That wouldn't work, right? Because in truth every Mushroomer believes he is sane.

I haven't been out in the world much, as far as I can remember at least. So I can't really judge. But it seems like Carolus's idea was sinister and effective. Apparently, people aren't meant to tell the truth to each other.

My eyes start to see things clearer now, but the Scientist's image is still blurry. I guess it'll only be minutes until I see who he is. Am I supposed to think he is someone I know?

"And the truth shall set you free," the Pillar muses. "Free enough to kill one another."

"Stop looking at the world from that angle," I tell him.

"Soon there'll be no angle to see the world from, dear Alice." The Pillar sighs. "So tell me, Mr. Scientist, shouldn't lying be a cure for the truth?"

"It should," the Scientist says. "But even if I knew how to cook that kind of cure, how long would it take to reach everyone? The Hookah of Hearts have been sold for more than a year. I designed it to take effect about a year in. Let's say, hypothetically, I cook a cure of lying now. How will you give it to the people? How long will it take to work?"

"So all this adventure was for nothing?" I tell myself. "At least I saved the kids."

"And what world will they live in?" the Pillar muses. "Mr. Scientist, there must be a cure."

I know this tone from the Pillar. He is planning on threatening this man once he retrieves his full vision like me.

And here we go. I can almost see everything in its normal size. Including the Scientist.

But this isn't quite right, because the Scientist is one of the Reds. I can't see his face wearing the cloak.

The Pillar, back to normal too, steps forward to pull the cloak, but is immediately stopped by the many other Reds squeezed into this room.

"I wouldn't come near me again if I were you," the Scientist says from under his cloak. "Let's keep it that way."

My first impression is not to struggle with those Reds. Because let's think about it. Something here isn't right.

"Then I assume you have nothing against us leaving." The Pillar flips his cane and pretends he's walking away.

"Not so fast, Senor Pillardo."

The words send a surge of fear through me. Is that the Executioner?

Chapter 64

Queen's garden, Buckingham Palace, London

"**A**nd the beauty of this plague is that it doesn't affect Wonderlanders," the Queen continued telling Margaret, "along with most of the South American cities where it was cooked. Fantastic-ballastic!" The Queen hailed.

"Does that mean that ordinary people can't handle the truth?" one of the guards asked curiously.

"Yes. Of course. Those two-faced hypocrite humans." The Queen grinned, then her face dimmed all of a sudden, sneering at the guard. "Who gave you permission to speak in the first place? Off with his head!"

Margaret watched the guards take him to execution, not really caring for him. "But truth or no truth, My Queen. We need to find a cure."

"No, we don't. I changed my mind," the Queen exclaimed. "The Jub Jub with the cure. I have a better idea."

"But you said—"

"Don't interrupt me, Margaret." Like a monkey, the Queen jumped on her chair again, pointing a finger straight into Margaret's eyes. "Forget everything I told you about sending someone after the Pillar."

"Forget about the Pillar?" Margaret thought the Queen had lost her mind—not that she possessed a healthy one in the first place.

"Yes, Margaret. I have a genius plan. One that, if it succeeds, will have me ruling the world."

Chapter 65

Brazil

The horror I see on the Pillar's face is scaring me.

And this time, there is no doubt about it. The Executioner is the Pillar's bogeyman, not matter how he tries to hide it.

"He doesn't die," one of the Reds answers in return. "The Scientist never dies."

"The Scientist is the Executioner?" I am thinking out loud.

The Reds laugh at me, enjoying it a lot. I want to shut them up and tell them they're nothing more than playing cards.

"That's impossible," the Pillar mumbles.

"Even if he didn't die in the explosion, why send us here?" I tell them.

"And why hide behind the cloak? It's not like him." The Pillar desperately wants to step closer, but is held back by the Reds.

"Maybe he's disfigured from the bomb. Besides, wasn't he depicted as a card with clubs for a head in Lewis Carroll's book?" I comment.

But no one answers me, not even the Pillar. A wicked silence fills the room for a while, and then one of the Reds nudges the Executioner, as if to permit him to talk.

Something isn't right, but I can't put my hands on it. I remind myself that we're wasting time here. We only have twenty-four hours left before the plague reaches irreversible measures like Carolus said on TV.

"It doesn't matter how I survived," the Executioner says from behind the darkness of his cloak. "I ordered the Reds to bring you to me for a reason."

"It's the key, right?" I say. "You want the Wonderland Key. I'll give it to you if you give me a cure." I'm lying, of course. I'll never give him the key, but I have to try my best. I realize it's funny that I'm lying to get to the truth.

"I don't want the key," the Executioner says. "At least not now."

"Then what do you want?" I am surprised the Pillar isn't talking. He keeps staring at the Executioner, wanting to pull off the hood.

"I want you to kill Carolus," the Executioner says.

"Why?" I ask.

"Because I lied to you. The plague is connected to Carolus's existence. Kill Carolus, and the world is cured."

Chapter 66

Alice's House, Oxford

The Cheshire watched Edith and Lorina Wonder locking themselves with their mother inside the house. The three of them seemed to have been some of the few people who'd never tried the Hookah of Hearts. And only those were the uninfected.

It had taken the Cheshire a long time to reach the Wonders' house. Not only was it the distance between London and Oxford, but he had to possess an infinite number of souls to get here. The driver, the old woman at the ticket booth, the police officer, and at some he'd had to possess a toddler when his mom turned out to be infected while the Cheshire was possessing her.

"Possessing you is a dirty job but somebody has to do it," he'd mumbled when he'd had to enter a rat's soul at the end of his ride.

But he stood outside the Wonders' house in a police officer's soul, peeking inside to take a better look at Lorina and Edith Wonder.

The two sisters were definitely on the dark side of evil. But were they who the Cheshire was looking for?

The problem with finding Tweedledum and Tweedledee was that, like Alice, none of them could remember their faces. Why? He had no idea.

All he remembered was how scary the twins were. Two lunatics walking through Wonderland. He also knew they were siblings. Brother and sister? Two brothers or two sisters? He couldn't remember.

Earlier, he had contacted someone who believed he knew who they were in this world, but that man turned out to be a liar. Now, the Cheshire roamed England, searching for the Tweedles.

Why the Tweedles?

Because only they and the Pillar were said to be able to enter Mushroomland and deal with the Executioner.

The Executioner who had once managed to chop off the Cheshire's head in Wonderland. If it wasn't for the Cheshire's knife right now, he'd be dead and gone.

He stuck his face to the window to take another look at Lorina and Edith. Could they be Tweedledum and Tweedledee?

They sure looked like it. But they weren't twins.

There was one way to find out. To possess one of them. Because the Cheshire, with all his powers, could never possess a Wonderlander.

Since neither of the sisters was going to open the door for anyone in this kill-fest outside, he had no choice but to possess another rat to get inside.

Yikes.

Chapter 67

Brazil

"Then why didn't you say so when we met in Mushroomland?" the Pillar demands, still held back by the Reds.

"What does it matter?" the Executioner says. "You want to stop the plague. I told you how to stop it."

"I'll call Inspector Dormouse." I pull out my phone. "I know he couldn't do it, but I'm sure there are excellent police officers who could if he contacted them."

"That won't work. Not just anyone can kill Carolus."

"I didn't know Carolus could be killed," the Pillar says. "He is a figment of Carroll's imagination."

"True. And only Lewis can kill him."

"So we're back to square one again," I say.

"He wouldn't have sent for us if that was all of it." The Pillar points his cane at the Executioner.

"Smart, Senor Pillardo." The Executioner laughs.

"Is he suggesting I go meet Lewis Carroll through the Tom Tower in London and ask him?" I turn to the Pillar. "We know the Tom Tower doesn't always work."

"No, Alice. I don't think it's that. He is suggesting that Lewis told you how to kill Carolus."

Hearing this, I close my eyes, trying to remember if he ever told me. But I am sure he didn't. "I hate to disappoint the world." I open my eyes. "But he didn't tell me how to kill Carolus."

"Of course he did," the Executioner says. "Carolus assured me Lewis told you how to kill him."

"He could have lied to you, just to let you think there was a cure," the Pillar suggests.

"I know a scared man when I see one, Senor Pillardo." The Executioner grunts at the Pillar, implying something about their past, which I suspect I will never know. "And Carolus shivered when I mentioned Alice to him."

In spite of the Executioner having denied my existence and trying to kill me in Mushroomland, I try to think of this as a confirmation that I am the Real Alice. Ironic how killing Lewis Carroll's split personality is the only way to find out now.

"So." The Pillar sighs. "I guess that's it. We know how to stop the plague. Come on, Alice. We have work to do."

"Is that it?" I wonder. "Don't you want to know how the Executioner survived?"

"Why would I? Clearly the man is invincible." The Pillar waves his hand. "Let's go."

Reluctantly, I follow his steps to the door, watching the Reds make room for us.

Then the Pillar pulls out his hookah, whips it at Reds, chokes a few of them, and heads straight toward the Executioner.

"Time for some None Fu," I say and begin the show.

Chapter 68

Carolus banged his head against the wall.

Part of it was the pain. But another part was his disappointment with the plan. He felt weakened needing to collaborate with the Queen of Hearts to get his medicine to relieve himself of the migraines.

This wasn't his plan at all.

Tomorrow was going to be the third day the plague had taken hold of the world. It was supposed to be the peak moment to execute his real plan. The real reason he had infected the world with his hookahs.

But now he'd become the Queen's slave, and she was going to use his weakness in her favor after their secret conversation in her chamber. She had an even more insane plan of her own now.

Not that he cared for her. All he needed was to play along until she gave him the Lullaby drug, and then, once the headaches were gone, he would proceed with his plan and force the Pillar to show himself.

For now, he has no choice but to wait, but no longer until tomorrow, or everything he'd planned would be gone with the wind.

Chapter 69

Brazil

The Reds aren't an easy fight, but my None Fu skills have progressed a lot.

I hit the first two Reds with straight kicks to their faces, which sends them both with their back against the wall. Then with two simultaneous fists, I punch their hollow faces underneath the cloaks. The first one drops into nothingness, leaving a red cloak lying on the floor behind him. The other, much stronger, strangles me with the fabric of his cloak, almost choking me.

Turned around now, I see the Pillar mass-finishing a few other Reds. I wish I'd learned to use that hose of his hookah. It's much more efficient than my yeeha-jumping techniques.

The Red choking me is too strong. I kick him with my legs and try to free myself from his grip with my hands, but it's all in vain. My choking noises are getting louder, like scattered vowels of lost words.

"You're saying something?" the Pillar says in the middle of his own fight. He strangles an attacking Red and then waves a hand behind his ears, pretending he can't hear what I'm saying. "Louder, Alice. Can't hear you."

I choke harder, now starting to lose my voice instead of getting louder. To top it off, another Red attacks me from the front. I stretch my legs against his chest to stop him from approaching. Now I'm squeezed between the two.

"That must be an awkward position you're in," the Pillar says, whipping his hose at other Reds. "Is that None Fu, too?"

My soul burns with revenge. I'm provoked like I have never been before. If I manage to kill the two Reds, it'll be mainly to prove to the Pillar I don't need him.

A crazy idea presents itself. I pull Lewis's key from my pocket and stretch my hand backward into the Red's face, attacking him with the small golden weapon.

Surprisingly, it works.

Well, kind of, as he sneezes red bubbles all over my hair and face. At least my neck is free now.

Freed from his grip, I land on the floor and pull the Red's cloak and bind it with the other Red's cloak in a heavy knot. The two mercenaries struggle to free themselves. No one must have done this to them before.

"Now that's None Fu," I tell the Pillar, kicking another Red in the face.

"See? I knew you could handle yourself. That's why I didn't help." He is about to pull off the Scientist's cloak when three of them strangle him from behind, pulling his hookah away.

"Need some help now?" I kick the Scientist in the back then hit his head, knocking him unconscious.

"Not in a million years," he says but struggles to free himself.

I use the Scientist's hand like a baseball bat and hit the first Red with it, then slap the other with the other hand. It's not much of a fight but enough distraction for the Pillar to handle the rest.

Then I plunge through the door, still pulling the Scientist's heavy body along.

Outside, it's pitch black. I don't have the slightest idea where we are. All I see is a silver Jeep parked at the curb. I keep pulling the Scientist, the Pillar still fighting inside.

The Scientist is a bit heavy, so it takes some time to sit him in the backseat. I kill a couple of Reds and then jump into the Jeep and ignite the engine.

I have no intention of waiting for the Pillar. Besides, I see a few attacking Reds in the distance. I push the pedal into the darkness, leaving the Pillar behind.

Chapter 70

With the fog lights on, I chug my way into some sort of jungle, with no idea where I'm heading.

The car bumps every other second. I squint, leaning forward, my chest on the wheel. For a moment, I wonder how I'm such a good driver. If so, why did I crash the school bus in the past?

It's only a few minutes before an army of Jeeps pops up behind me. Their lights are much stronger than mine. I feel like a thief exposed by the watchtower's light while trying to escape a prison.

The worst part is that I don't know where I am going. How can I contact the Pillar's chauffeur to pick me up?

"Hey, Scientist!" I shout at the back of my Jeep. "Wake up!"

I hear no reply from the comatose body in the back.

Instead, I hear the Reds in the Jeeps behind me. They're telling me to stop and give the Scientist back, or they'll let their animals loose after me.

Animals?

"Scientist! Wake up. How am I supposed to kill Carolus?"

This time, I get back a sort of response. A snore.

Then I hear the animals let loose behind me. They don't sound like dogs. I hear them treading the earth so loud my Jeep shakes. What kind of dogs are those?

Adjusting the rearview mirror while hitting another bump in the road, I see silhouettes of oversized animals, eager to eat a piece of me. They're panting, not like dog, but...wait...they're not panting.

They're roaring.

Am I being chased by lions?

"You still have a chance to stop!" one of the Reds says.

"And you have a chance to back off before I kill your precious Scientisto!" I roar back, mostly shaking when I see they're really lions in the rearview mirrors.

Not the usual lions you see at the zoo. These are a bit heavier. Fatter. Rounder. Dotted with black spots, and they have sharp, irregular teeth.

I let out the loudest shriek, my eyes bulging out, hardly gripping the wheel. I grip the wheel harder when I'm about to lose control of it.

It's the teeth that have me panicked.

I know those teeth. I've seen them before. They look like the Bandersnatch teeth in my bullets.

Chapter 71

The lions are so close they bump their heads against the back of my Jeep.

I wonder why this Scientist hasn't woken up yet. I didn't hit him that hard, did I?

Clutching the pedal to its max, a light suddenly appears in the sky.

Finally, the Pillar's chopper.

I hear the kids rooting for me up there. "Alice save us!"

"Alice needs someone to save her," I mumble, trying not to think about the lion running parallel to my Jeep now.

"I'm throwing you a rope to pick you up!" the chauffeur says, as a rope dangles before my eyes.

"I need two. I have to bring the Scientist along. He must know more than what he has told us."

"I only have one rope. Attach him to it, and I will send it down to you again!"

"How am I supposed to attach him to the rope while driving?" I scream.

I pull my umbrella and squeeze it between the chair and the clutch so the Jeep keeps speeding, then grip the rope and jump in the back. There is a metal belt that I bind to the Scientist's body, and then I tell the chauffeur to pull it up.

Another lion slashes his paws at me in an acrobatic move, and I fall back to the driver's seat.

"I'm sending it back!" the chauffeur shouts.

That's the same instant when the car starts slowing down.

"No!"

One look at the dashboard, and I realize I'm out of fuel.

In a flash, I grip the rope and begin to tighten the belt around my waist. For some reason, it's not working. It won't click closed.

"It's not working!"

"That's not good."

"No shit. I know it's not good."

"No, Alice, you don't understand," the kids shout. "There is a cliff ahead of you."

"This is some Hollywood movie I'm in," I mumble again. "Lions, Reds, and a cliff. All I need is an earthquake."

The Jeep keeps slowing down, and one of lions manages to jump inside.

I can't even scream now. I don't remember Alice in Wonderland dying in Wonderland.

The belt finally clicks and I tell them to pull me up.

The lions snatches my shoe away then pulls on the tip of my jeans. He could easily have my feet for an appetizer now, but I guess he's into the whole meal.

Embarrassed, I have no choice but to pull off my jeans, but not before I pull out the key and tuck it between my teeth.

I stare at the roaring lions and the maddening Reds below me, and let out a sigh.

But it's not long before the Reds start laughing hysterically at me. The kids too.

Damn my pink underwear, shining bright in the dark of the Brazilian jungle.

Chapter 72

Up in the plane, the children welcome me and give me a blanket to cover my legs until further notice.

"Thank you," I tell the chauffeur.

"You're welcome," a voice answers.

Then the Pillar appears out of the cockpit. He smiles and high fives a few kids.

"How did you get here?" I say.

"I stepped through the door," he winks. "Never had a thing for entering a plane through a window."

"Pillar!"

"Ah, you mean, how did I fight hordes of Reds on my own without even staining my suit with their blood?" He rubs a feather off his sleeve. "I've always had a thing for staying clean and tidy, right children?"

"Pillar clean!" They raise their hands.

"Besides," the Pillar continues, "if I hadn't survived, you wouldn't have been saved from the Reds." He leans back into his favorite couch and presses a button. A screen of the beach rolls down behind him, and sounds of chirping birds fill the plane.

One of the kids strolls over, wearing an ice cream man outfit. "Ice Cream. Banana flavor. Mango flavor. Even strawberry. One penny each."

The Pillar leans forward and tips the boy, rewarding himself with an ice cream crone. "Ice cream, kids?" he turns to the others.

"Yeah!"

It's a shame I'm drooling over the ice cream in this humid oven of a chopper.

"Ice cream, Alice?" He smiles.

I sneer at him.

"And, please, no need to thank me for saving your pink butt."

The children can't stop laughing, their noses stained with some red strawberry flavor.

"I had to leave you behind." I stick out my neck. "The same way you betrayed me in the Garden of Cosmic Speculation."

"You left me?" The Pillar pouts like a bratty child. "I'm shocked. I thought you had to save the Scientist and didn't have the chance to think about me."

"Stop playing with my head. You know I left you on purpose."

"But you're glad that I'm alive, right?" he says. "Come on, aren't you children glad I'm alive?"

The children gather around him, some of them kissing him. I wonder why they like him so much. It's as if they're sharing a special connection I can't put my hands on. The same way I sensed he and the Executioner kept a secret.

"Are you glad I'm alive, my chauffeur?" He cranes his neck at the cockpit.

"Of course, Professor. I need someone to tell me how to drive this plane properly."

We hit another air bump.

"Watch out for those clouds you keep bumping into." The Pillar raises his ice cream cone.

"It's not a cloud, Professor," I hear the chauffeur snicker from inside the cockpit. "It's a big mushroom in the sky."

The kids laugh at this, too. Suddenly I'm the most boring person on set. But I don't care. It's time for the next step in stopping the plague.

"I think we better know who the Scientist really is." I point at the comatose body on the plane's floor.

Chapter 73

"First I need to know where I'm going," the chauffeur interrupts.

"London, of course," the Pillar says. "Alice needs to find Carolus and kill him."

"Oki doki!"

"I'm still not sure how I'm the one who's supposed to kill him." I say.

"I'm not sure either. But I believe the Scientist. He didn't tell us this last precious detail until we pushed him hard."

"Yes, but how? I mean, just shoot him?"

"I really doubt the likes of Carolus will die that easily. If only Alice can kill Lewis Carroll's split persona, then there has to be a certain method to do it. Didn't Lewis ever tell you how when you met him?"

"Not that I remember."

"I guess he only wanted to give you the key." The Pillar eyes it in my hand. I grip it harder. "Don't worry. I won't take it from you. We need the Six Keys all together anyway. I have one. You have one. That's about fair."

"Lewis told me not to show it to you in particular, in case you want to know."

"I don't." He dismisses me. "But I do want to know how you can kill Carolus before tomorrow night, or the world will be toast."

"And how am I supposed to find that out?"

"Well, let's start with the Scientist, the Executioner, or whoever he is." The Pillar walks toward the body, about to pull the hood back. "I'm sure he hasn't told us everything. Nice pants by the way."

I sneer at him. "Aren't all Reds just hollow underneath the cloak?"

"He isn't a Red, that's for sure." He grips the hood.

"How do you know?"

"Didn't you see how the Reds nudged him to make him talk or stop talking?" the Pillar says. "My assumption is the Scientist was their prisoner. They just wanted us to think otherwise for some reason."

"So pull it off, then."

"Are you ready, children?" He acts like a magician again.

Along with the children, I nod eagerly.

Then he pulls the hood back.

It's not the Executioner, and I am not surprised. I had a feeling the Reds were lying to scare us.

But I never guessed it would be The March Hare.

Chapter 74

Queen's garden, Buckingham Palace, London

The Queen wouldn't tell Margaret her new plan, and she enjoyed how it drove the Duchess crazy.

"Tell me, Margaret. Aren't the world's presidents having a meeting in the United Nations Office at Geneva?"

"Yes, tomorrow afternoon. Why?"

"I want to attend it."

"But you declined the invitation earlier."

"That was when I was concerned with stopping Carolus from ending the world."

"What's changed? His plague is still going to end the world. We haven't found a cure."

"You won't understand, Margaret. You know why? Because you're ugly."

"It's dumb people who usually don't understand." Margaret folded her arms.

The Queen knew how much Margaret hated her but couldn't oppose her, not before they found the keys. She enjoyed such suppression a lot, even better than painting white roses red.

"Well, then we're about to change that," the Queen said. "Once this plague is over, teachers should tell students that it's ugly people who don't understand, and that dumb people only look horrible. Now back to what I was saying."

"All ears, My Queen."

"Get me on a plane to Geneva to meet up with the presidents of the world tomorrow. Remind me, what was the meeting about?"

"The plague, of course." Margaret sighed. "The world's only concern at the moment. They're looking for a solution."

"Of course, I knew that, Margaret. Did you think I was dumb—I mean ugly like you?" The Queen grinned.

"And what about Carolus, if I may ask?"

"He's coming with me." The Queen prided herself. "Those presidents of the world have no idea what I have prepared for them. It's so amazing I feel taller already!"

Chapter 75

The Pillar's Chopper

"Professor Jittery?" I cup my hands over my mouth.

The March Hare snaps out of his sleep, stretching his arms out like a blind man. "Where am I?"

"Relax." The Pillar knocks his butt with his cane. "You're on my plane."

I sneer at the Pillar and take the March Hare in my arms to calm him down. I have no idea how he is the Scientist, but I still feel for him since we met in the Hole. One look at him and you realize he is nothing but a child in an old man's body.

"Oh, I remember now," he rubs his head. "You hit me on the head, Alice."

"I had to, so I could bring you here with me. You have no idea what kind of adventure we had while you were unconscious. I still can't believe you're the Scientist. Why would you do such a horrible thing like cooking this plague?"

"Because he wants to go back to Wonderland." The Pillar stands over us, about to pull the March's long hair and smash him into the wall, I think.

"Is that true?" I pat the March Hare, who's still shivering in my hands.

"It's complicated."

"Explain it to me, please." I say.

"As if we have all the time in the world." The Pillar looks at his pocket watch.

"Two years ago, Carolus visited me in the Hole," the March begins. "I had no idea how he got in, let alone how he escaped Wonderland. I even thought he was Lewis in the beginning."

I turn to look at the Pillar.

"It happened a lot in Wonderland. People mistook Carolus for being Carroll," he says. "We didn't even know about Carroll's split persona for some time."

"Okay. Tell me more, Jittery."

"Carolus promised me he'd get me out of the Hole in exchange for cooking the plague, which he knew about from meeting Nobody in Peru," the March says. "I said no."

"I know you're a scientist, among other things," I say. "But why would Carolus think you could cook this unusual plague?"

"Because of a plant I accidentally came across in the Garden of Cosmic Speculation."

"A plant that makes one tell the truth?" I ask.

"In the strangest ways," the March says. "I think it's not from this world, but from Wonderland. It must have crossed over somehow when one of those portals opened."

"Cut the chit-chat, and get to the meat of the matter," the Pillar says.

"I refused Carolus's offer, although he was too tense that day, suffering from his migraines as usual. He offered to bring me back to Wonderland, but I still refused because I knew he was lying to me."

"How can you be sure?" I say.

"Think of it. Lewis Carroll was never trapped in Wonderland, and neither was his split persona. Lewis was the one who locked most of the monsters in," the March says. "Lastly, Carolus made me an offer I couldn't refuse."

"What was it?"

Just as the March is about to tell me, we hear the sound of another engine in the air.

"Who's following us?" the Pillar asks his chauffeur.

"The Reds!"

And they are starting to shoot at us, midair.

Chapter 76

"What was the offer you couldn't refuse?" The Pillar aggressively pulls the March by his ears.

"He offered to help me get rid of the one thing that made the Reds follow us up here in the air." the March cries.

"You mean some kind of a detector?" the Pillar says.

"No." The March's eyes dart upwards. "The light bulb in my head. The one Black Chess installed to know what I'm thinking about."

The Pillar sighs, his neck stretching as he stares up at the ceiling. His stare is so intense that I feel the need to protect the March. The sound of showering bullets outside makes things worse.

"Guess what, kiddo," the Pillar tells the March. "If Black Chess had access to that light bulb in your head, they'd have known how to stop the plague, because they have no use for a disease that will end the world for good like that."

The March's ears tense in the Pillar's hands, and at the same time I hug the kids, worried they'll get hit with the bullets. "Have you ever had a light bulb in your head?" the March grunts back.

The Pillar says nothing.

"Then you have no idea what you're talking about." The March pulls away from the Pillar's grip, not like a strong man would do, but like an angry child. "What you're not paying attention to is what is really going on, Pillar!"

The March spits all over the Pillar's face.

"Tell us, March." I squeeze the Pillar's hand. "Tell us the whole story. Why did you pretend you're with the Reds? I noticed they nudged you to tell us the things you told us in that room in Brazil."

"I'd better help my chauffeur with firing at the Reds." The Pillar disappears into the cockpit, although I know he can hear us from there.

"After I cooked him his plague, Carolus betrayed me," the March says. "That was two years ago. I didn't see the point in telling you when you visited me, because the plague wasn't known to the public then."

"I understand."

"Three days ago, he kidnapped me from the Hole and hired the Reds to imprison me in Brazil."

"So the Pillar was right. Everything you told us down there was influenced by the Reds."

"They drugged me with a different plant that forced me to say whatever they told me to say, and they were secretly threatening me with a knife, but none of you noticed."

"And the Executioner part?"

"That was the Pillar's suggestion because he always feared the Executioner, so we went with the flow, letting you believe whatever you wanted to believe."

"What was the point of all of this?"

"I don't know," the March says. "I don't think even the Reds know. But it was all Carolus's plan."

"Which means he knew we'd end up in Brazil. How about the part about only me being capable of killing him? I'm not sure that's even true." I face the March Hare again. "Or?"

"Actually, that's the one thing that is true," the March explains. "If you remember, I only told you this part later in the conversation when the effect of their drug was wearing off. It still hasn't completely."

"And that's all you remember?"

"For now. I'm sure I'll remember more when it wears off completely," the March says. "But the part of killing him, I heard it when one of the Reds was talking to him on the phone yesterday."

"But you didn't hear how I can kill him?"

"Sorry, no. They didn't discuss it."

"Let's say this is true. How is killing Carolus going to stop the plague?"

"There is only one explanation," the March says. "That I cooked it that way."

"Is that possible?"

"It is, but I can't remember if I did. Why would I cook a plague that can only be stopped when Carolus dies?"

Chapter 77

"Look." The Pillar returns, rubbing off powder from his suit. "This whole story doesn't make sense. I know this kiddo isn't lying." He points at the March Hare. "Because I know he's one of the Inklings. But whatever Carolus staged for us, there is something that doesn't make sense."

"And?" I say.

"Your only hope is that you get back to London and kill Carolus."

"Even if I do, I don't know how."

"I'm sure you do, Alice."

"I don't. Stop counting on me that much. There are things that I don't know."

"You know more than you think." The Pillar steps up. "Like the key Carroll gave you and you didn't tell me about. Try to remember. He must have given you a clue how to kill his split persona.

"He didn't even mention it."

"Well, then let's have a tea party here on the plane with this loon and his light bulb and watch the world end from above." The Pillar steps away and starts rummaging through some stuff. "I hope we have enough fuel to last after the end of the world."

"All right," I snap. "I will try my best to kill Carolus."

"Good girl." He pulls out two machine guns.

"But first, I need to send the kids to Fabiola to take care of."

The Pillar stops, stares back at the kids, that serene smile flashing again. I think those kids are the only ones he smiles at that way. I wish I could know more about his connection to them. "Of course," he says. "Although the Vatican is already a mess. I'm hoping Fabiola can accommodate you safely in her church."

"So to the Vatican first?" asks the chauffeur.

I nod at him.

"Oh, God. I miss Fabiola so much." The March Hare claps his hands.

The Pillar looks back into his guns and straps on a backpack.

"And where are you going?" I grimace.

"Get closer to the Reds' plane and open the back of the plane," the Pillar shouts at the chauffeur. He stares at me with admiration as the back door slides open. "It was nice meeting you, Alice."

The air swirls like angry ghosts into the plane, as the Pillar puts on his goggles.

"I have a war of my own," he says, turns around, and jumps midair onto the Reds' plane, which is a little lower than ours.

The door slides back to a close. All of us are totally astonished.

"Where is he going?" I ask the chauffeur.

"To hell, my dear Alice." The chauffeur nods. "To hell and back."

Chapter 78

The Reds' Plane

"Is that the Pillar who just jumped on our plane?" Ace, the leader of the Reds said.

"It's him, Ace." said number Three.

"So he's about to do it?"

"It's looks like it," said number Three. "It was inevitable, if you ask me."

"Bring my parachute," Ace ordered. "I'd get your parachute too, if I were you."

"So we're abandoning the mission?"

"We've done all Carolus asked of us," Ace said. "He wanted us to bring him Alice, and I believe she is on her way to London now. Our job is done."

"And the Pillar?"

"We should be all gone when he enters the plane," Ace said. "His war isn't with us."

"I heard he's unstoppable when he's angry." Number Three said, strapping up. "You said his war isn't with us, Sir. May I ask who the Pillar's real enemy is in his war?"

"His past, number three," Ace said, and jumped out, leaving the rain of bullets attacking the plane behind.

The Pillar had arrived.

Chapter 79

Radcliffe asylum, Oxford

A rat, with a cell phone between its teeth, scurried its way through the sewers into the asylum.

"That's the worst thing that has happened to me, possessing a rat's body twice in one day," the Cheshire thought.

First he had possessed Edith's body in the Wonders' house to make sure she and her sister weren't the Tweedles, but then they proved to be ordinary useless humans like others.

Now, he was getting curiouser and curiouser.

He scurried farther among the Mushroomers who'd spotted him and tried to slap him dead with their shoes.

Some rats die in the worst ways, he thought again. Had any of those ugly humans ever thought how it'd feel being killed under a giant shoe? And what happened when the first hit didn't kill the rat. Were they going to finish their kill with another hit?

Not that the Cheshire liked rats. As a cat, he sometimes ate them, although he thought they tasted awful. What did you expect from something that lived in sewers?

But he'd stand up for a rat against any human on any given day.

Still scurrying away, his phone rang in his teeth. He shuddered to the vibration and decided enough was enough.

He possessed a Mushroomer and stooped over to pick up the phone from the rat he'd once possessed.

"Yes?"

"It's Margaret."

"I'm still looking for Tweedledee and Tweedledum," he said, seeing that none of the other Mushroomers paid attention to him. Now that was the beauty of living among insane folks. They wouldn't give attention to such a sentence like the one he'd just uttered.

"I don't think that's necessary now. Plans have changed."

"I've almost lost one of my nine lives in my quest, and you tell me plans have changed?"

"The Queen is about to make things worse with one of her stupid plans again."

"What? She decided to cut off the headless horseman's head?"

"Worse. We're on our way to the UN headquarters in Geneva. We're meeting with the presidents of the world."

"Got an appetite for some sightseeing while the world is going down?"

"The presidents of the world are supposedly discussing how to deal with the plague."

"I bet that's a camouflage for something else."

"They're actually planning how to get the elite people of the world to escape if the world really ends tomorrow," Margaret said. "They will even have part of the fake conference broadcasted on TV, but that's not the issue."

"I think I know what the issue is. The Queen is about to turn this conference upside down somehow."

"Yes. She wouldn't tell me how, but what worries me is that she and Carolus became friends all of a sudden."

"That's wonderfully weird in a very sinister way."

"I think he told her a secret about the plague that we don't know of, and they made a deal of some kind. I don't know what it is."

"Frankly, I don't care. I'd be happy to see everyone in the world die, and I have nine lives. I wouldn't mind living in this world, although it means I'd end up possessing rats and cockroaches."

"I think you better come to Geneva, Cheshire. I have to go now."

The Cheshire hung up, not really caring about what the Queen had in mind. He'd come here to find the Tweedles, which he thought was a fun pursuit. If it wasn't Edith and Lorina, then he suspected it'd be Dr. Tom Truckles children. The Twins. Todd and Tania.

And he was about to find out. Only one thing stopped him now. He realized that as a Mushroomer, he was locked behind bars now. How he wished he hadn't let that rat go.

Chapter 80

"**G**et in, children," Fabiola urges them.

I make sure the March Hare and chauffeur get in safe as well. The world outside in the piazza has gone bonkers. The basilica is the last resort for the uninfected at the moment. The early morning twilight slants through its dome, reminding me I have less than twenty-four hours to kill Carolus.

"Where is the Pillar?" Fabiola asks.

"He jumped out of the plane," I say. "I have no idea why."

"Good." She took the March Hare in her arms. "Missed you, buddy. Really missed you."

"I love you, White Queen. It's been so long. I want to go back to Wonderland."

"Someday, March. Someday."

Watching the old March playing child and mother with Fabiola is a bit strange. I like the March. I can feel the purity of his heart when I talk to him, but how is he supposed to be an asset to the Inklings?

The children gather around Fabiola as well.

Fabiola is like a universal language. Every color, ethnicity, and gender throw themselves in her arms. She is like a light at the end of a dark tunnel. It's either the fear of the dark or the freedom of light in arms.

I sit next to a few uninfected in the church, watching Fabiola organize everything. She makes sure all entrances are perfectly locked, that there is food for everyone, and that no one has gotten infected somehow while inside.

"You did a great job, Alice," she tells me. "I'm repeatedly impressed by your insistence to make the world better."

"Thank you," I say. "It was a bit of a darker ride in Columbia, however."

"I know." She holds my hands. "The Executioner?"

"How come there are such bad people in the world?"

"I don't specialize in analyzing bad people. I prefer to look for the good in people and help them bring it out. It's a better way to look at the world."

"Not with the Pillar, I guess."

She almost lowers her gaze. "The Pillar is a man who often has the chance to be good yet prefers to walk the other side." Her voice is a bit shattered. "I feel no salvation for him."

Well, putting it that way makes sense. I have to admit I am confused about him, but she just described my problem with him exactly. Every time I fall for his charm or sarcastic look at the world, he throttles me back with a bad move.

"He fooled me into showing him where I had hidden one of the keys last week," I say.

"I heard he posed as the Mad Hatter," she says.

I lower my head. Heroes shouldn't be fooled that easily.

"It's all right, but you should know he was going to give it to the Queen of Hearts."

"How do you know?"

"I have my sources. He made a deal with her and Black Chess."

"So he's working with them now?"

"I don't think so. All I know is he promised the Queen to get her the key in exchange of something. And like I told you before: the Pillar is not on anyone's side but his own."

"Are you telling me he shouldn't be part of the Inklings at all costs?"

"I'm telling you that you should search the Inklings tile by tile when this is over to make sure he didn't buy it for a reason of his own," Fabiola says. "The least I can imagine is that he'd like to know what you're planning."

"You really need to tell me more about him sometime, Fabiola."

"When the right time comes. So I take it that you didn't get the key back yet. It's important that you do."

"Not yet. I saw him with it and was planning to get it back when we returned, but then he jumped out of the plane in Brazil."

"Brazil?" Fabiola tilts her head and looks back at the kids. "Did you get those kids from Brazil?"

"No, Columbia. They were slaves for the Executioner."

"Oh, my God, how didn't I see it?" Fabiola runs back to the kids and kneels down to check their hands. Once she sees they're missing two fingers, she hugs them tighter, tears forming in her eyes.

"Is there something I should know about those kids?" I stand helpless, a bit too irritated with so many truths being kept from me.

"No." She wipes off her tears. "You did good, Alice." She pulls me closer with one arm and hugs me as well. "Damn you, Pillar, for opening up those old wounds."

"I'm sorry, Fabiola, but I think I deserve to know what's going on."

"You want to know what's going on?" she sobs between the kids' shoulders. "I know now why the Pillar pretended he was the Hatter and stole the keys from you last week."

Chapter 81

The Executioner's men had no warning.

Still mourning the death of their leader, they were about to have a meeting to elect a new one. Millions of dollars, drug money, was about to come in this week, and someone had to lead the way. And since they had lost too many children to this Alice girl, they had to plan to kidnap and enslave more children soon. Poor children, orphans, were their best candidates.

But none of this went as planned.

Why?

Because of the man in the blue suit with white stripes and golden buttons. The man in the hat with a little bit of bad skin as if it was about to peel off. The man with the hookah who always wore white gloves.

At first, he looked like a silly magician out of a Hollywood movie or something, getting out that plane with two machine guns in his hands and strings of bullets on his back.

Although they had seen him earlier, quirky and full of life, he had turned into a man with no expression on his face. A dull look, heartless and uncaring.

The Pillar shot left and right. Up and ahead. No mercy. No second thought. Not wincing for a moment. Not retreating.

Blood spattered all around and on his suit. He didn't care.

On his face. He didn't notice it.

He loaded his guns again and walked like Clint Eastwood shooting left and right.

None of them had a chance to match his skill.

Those who were new in the business wondered who this man was. How he had acquired such skills, and how in the name of mushrooms and grins he dared infiltrate Mushroomland.

But those who'd been here for a long time knew him well. Those were the ones who began running first, although he chased them one by one and finished them.

Those were the ones who knew his name. Senor Pillardo, who had once been one of them.

Everyone had feared Senor Pillardo, but why he was shooting at them now remained a mystery to all.

One of the last survivors, lying panting on the grass, saw the Pillar standing among the piles of dead drug traffickers. He watched him retreat back to his plane, about to take off.

Suddenly the dying man knew him. "You're..." he stuttered. "It can't be!" he watched the Pillar taking off, and knew that the man in the blue suit wasn't finished yet.

Chapter 82

St Peter's, The Vatican

Fabiola doesn't tell me why the Pillar took the key. She doesn't tell me what's so special about those children. And it drives me crazy.

I can't force her to tell me. The White Queen has this kind of aura that makes you trust her, no matter what. If she decided not to tell me she must have a good reason for it.

I watch Fabiola spend most of her time taking special care of the Columbian children – I realize not all of them are Columbian, but from all over the world -- while the March Hare tries to remember more about the plague.

"What boggles my mind is how I could cook such a plague." He trotted across the church left and right.

"What do you mean?" I ask.

"I mean, no matter what Carolus promised me, or forced me to do, I could never have designed something that could hurt anyone in the world. It's just not me."

I believe him.

"You think he drugged me so I had no control of myself?"

"I don't know." I shake my shoulders. "Maybe you're like him and have a split persona."

"That would be horrible." He brushes his long beard. "I don't think I'm horrible. Do you think I'm horrible?"

"Calm down."

"I think I have to." His eyes shot up again. "I think my light bulb flickered."

I don't know what to say.

"Perhaps I shouldn't think much or someone will see my thoughts. Fabiola, do you think I can hide in your confession booth?"

"If it'll make you feel better." She approached me. "So still no idea how you will kill Carolus?"

"I went through all my meetings with Lewis and I still have no idea." I look at my watch. "Shouldn't you know something?"

"Why do you say that?"

"I don't mean to interfere, but you looked like you were intimate in the vision I had about the Six Inklings."

Fabiola looks like she's suppressing a smile. "Well, he always talked about your umbrella. He liked that gadget, the same way he liked the Vorpal sword he gave me."

"I remember that." I chuckle. "I'd love to see you chop off bad guys' heads with it again."

"Don't count on it. I've devoted my life to peace. That was the Pillar's effect that day. He makes people dip into their dark sides. He's good at it."

"So what about the umbrella?"

"Maybe it's the Bandersnatch teeth bullets, or the way it glowed when you shot the Cheshire with it in the cat throwing festival."

"You think so?"

"It's our last chance."

All right." I sigh. "I'll have the chauffeur fly me to London."

"Wait!" The chauffeur strolls over and shows us video footage from his phone.

"What is it?"

"It's Senor Pillardo—I mean the Pillar."

Chapter 83

BBC Report

A man in a blue suit seems to have succeeded in doing what no government has ever been able to accomplish.

The unnamed hero, flying an uncharted plane, raided all of the Columbian drug locations in as little as one hour. Reports are still unclear how he did this, but some locals say they saw him kill each and every member of the drug cartels owned by the infamous criminal called the Executioner. Locals reported seeing this man on his own with two machine guns, on foot, shooting them left and right.

Then, a few minutes later, he bombed Mushroomland, where the most expensive drugs were grown.

"This man come. Shoot all bad men. No mercy. One time," one of the locals says. "He shoot. They die. Simple. He Jesus Christ machine gun."

Another older Columbian woman says, "I see movie Men in Black. Good guys. Shoot aliens. This man better. He is man in blue. Shoot. Kill. No reply."

"I have to admit I have never seen such a daring human being, reported an Englishman living in Columbia. "I mean he was Rambo on mushrooms. Terminator on crack. He shot them with uncanny accuracy, said nothing, got back on his plane, burned everyone else."

The same instant the world is trying to survive the most lethal plague in history, a single man ends the reign of the drug cartels. Maybe he is part superman, wearing blue. Maybe he is heaven-sent to save us. In any case, maybe there is still hope in this world.

Chapter 84

St Peter's, The Vatican

All of us watch the news in awe.

The children clap their hands, most enthusiastic about it, although I am against them watching it. It is Fabiola who insists they do. I can't understand what the deal is with the children yet.

"Why did he go back to do this?" I ask Fabiola.

"You never know what's on the Pillar's mind." She looks away. She is lying. She knows why. I'm starting to lose my patience.

"In spite of all his bad doings, he rid the world of those bad people."

"Did he?" She looks back. "Or did he just promote more violence in the world?"

I am confused. She has a point, but the Pillar may also have a point.

"Do you know of a reason why he would go back to do this while we're in the middle of stopping Carolus?" I ask her.

"I have no idea, Alice. You said it yourself. He went back when you needed him. Trust me. He just wants to evoke chaos. And even if he doesn't, you'll figure out he has an agenda of his own. I hope he returns and gives you back his key."

"You're right," I say, trying to keep my focus on what matters. "I suppose I will let the chauffeur fly back to London."

"We'll have to delay that a bit," the chauffeur says. "The chopper needs some maintenance. But not for long. Don't worry."

"Besides, you won't find Carolus in London," Fabiola says.

"What do you mean?"

"My sources have told me the Queen of Hearts captured him and is taking him with her to the UN's meeting in Geneva."

"Geneva? The Queen and Carolus? Something isn't right here."

"I know. That's is why you have to kill him sooner. Who knows what the Queen has planned for us all."

Chapter 85

Since the Cheshire couldn't find another rat to possess, he resorted to a fly in the end.

Now this was risky business.

For one, he had to leave his phone behind for good now. Second, he was prone to getting killed any moment. Humans loved to kill flies.

To tell the truth, it was tempting, like killing ants. Just a calculated slap and the fly was history.

But soon he found himself another host. One of the asylum's wardens.

The Cheshire strolled through the ward like had before when he possessed Ogier's body and scared this Alice girl a few weeks ago. Oh, boy, was that fun. That look on her face would have made one hell of a selfie.

But enough with that poor girl thinking she was the Real Alice. It was Tom's kids he was looking for.

He gestured at a few other wardens on his way. Everyone seems concerned with something called Plan-X. This loon Dr. Truckle thought he'd survive apocalypse in this asylum.

But frankly, what did the Cheshire care? All these humans, dumb as a bum.

And here he was, staring at Tom's children, Todd and Tania, with that famous Cheshire grin on his lips.

The two obnoxious kids stared back. There weren't scared of him. Not at all. They grinned back.

Although he'd heard the news about the Pillar and Alice leaving Columbia by now, and the Queen's disinterest in sending someone after the Pillar by now, the Cheshire felt excited, staring at Todd and Tania.

I bet I found you after all Tweedledee and Tweedledum. This will be fun.

Chapter 86

St Peter's, The Vatican

The March Hare, still hiding in the confession booth, watched the few uninfected people sitting outside. They were waiting for Fabiola's return. She had taken Alice and the children and went to check on that plane they were talking about with that mousy man who called himself the chauffeur.

During their wait, a priest entered the room.

The March could only see him from behind. He was watching him stand behind the podium, about to talk to the people, who were dead silent. The March wondered if it was out of respect or fear of the man at the podium.

One thing was definitely odd about this priest. He smoked a cigar.

"Hallelujah!" the man said. "All you lazy obnoxious sin washers."

The March's eyes widened. The uninfected people stiffened in their places.

"Seriously," said the priest. "Is this all you can do when the shit hits the wall?"

The March was confused. Was that Carolus in the priest's outfit?

"All you whining, crying, wailing wusses of the world." The priest raised both arms. "Going to church, your arches bent over, your heads lowered, and your whole existence just a mess."

The uninfected looked extremely offended.

"Is that all you can do? No wonder each villain in this world is treading on your sorry existence, making money out of you, poisoning your food, and just toying with you left and right."

The March thought this couldn't be Carolus now. This man was shorter, and he thought he recognized the voice.

"Forgive me father for I have sinned," the priest mocked them, dangling out his tongue. "Sinned? Really? You? Have you ever really been introduced to sin? What did you do? Lie to your spouse? Seen a crime and not told about it? Were late for work? Tell me. What was your worst sin ever?"

The March recognized the voice now.

"Have you ever killed someone with your bare hands and hated it?" The priest walked sideways. The March saw he was all soaked in blood, still smoking his cigar. "Have you ever stared evil in the face and grinned at it? Have you ever met a villain? A real one who kills for grins and giggles? Have you ever been kidnapped as a child and sent to work for drug lords on the other side of the world? Have you ever met the darker side of yourself like Lewis Carroll did? Have you ever had to deal with it over and over again, and swear you'd never pass it on to the world, but write the all-time best children's book instead?"

The uninfected looked rather embarrassed, that March could see.

"If I were you, I would feel ashamed for the rest of your life," The priest looked around. "If I were you, I wouldn't hide in here and cry and pray for someone to save my sorry butt because I think I'm a good person. If I were you, I'd turn and face the villain."

The March's ears stood erect, seeing how some of them had been influenced by the priest's talk, about to push the church's gates open and deal with the plague.

"Go out now! Stare darkness in the face and kick its ass!"

Just before they did, the March Hare saw Fabiola enter the church, yelling at the priest. "How dare you come in here with that blood on your hands and talk to them like that?" she roared like he'd never seen her for a long time. "Get out of here, Pillar!"

Chapter 87

St Peter's, The Vatican

When I get back to the basilica, I see Fabiola scream at the Pillar.

I don't actually hear most of what she says. I am looking at the Pillar. He takes off the fake priest's outfit, showing the blood-stained blue suit underneath. His face is slashed with bruises and cuts, and he needs medical attention.

More than anything, he looks like someone who needs a hug to me. You can't kill so many people and feel okay, not even if you are the Pillar.

"I want you gone." I hear Fabiola now. "I don't want to see you ever again."

"Why would you say something like that to me?" He sounds sincere.

"You're a terrible man." The veins on her neck stick out. "A terrible, terrible man. Get out."

"I just killed everyone who worked for the Executioner, Fabiola. Does that not count as an act of righteousness to you?"

"You don't want justice, Pillar. All you want is blood."

"How can you have justice without blood?"

Wow. The conversation is taking a heavy turn.

"Ask the kids," he approached them. "Are you happy the Executioner and his friends are all dead now?"

The kids hurray.

"Stay away from them." Fabiola stands in the way. "They don't need a role model like you in their lives."

"Yeah, I understand." The Pillar wipes blood off his lips. "I'm the bad guy after all."

"Don't try to have anyone sympathize with you," Fabiola says. "You fooled Alice and took the key from her. You made a deal with the Queen of Hearts."

"I did."

"Why?" I cut in. "Why give the key back to her?"

"First of all, I have the key with me. I haven't given it to her yet."

"So why were you going to give it to her after you played me?"

"I said I made a deal. I didn't say I was going to keep my end of it."

Chapter 88

"I don't understand," I say.

"The Queen asked to meet me a few days earlier, asking me if I'd join Black Chess," the Pillar says. "I said no, but then she offered to tell me the whereabouts of the Executioner, which she knew was very important to me. I've been looking for the Executioner for so long—don't ask me why."

"See?" Fabiola says. "He only stands on *his* side."

"Wait, Fabiola, please." I sense I'm about to hear something else that I don't like. "Does this mean we weren't in Columbia to find the cure?"

The Pillar hesitates. "No. I brought you along so you could help the children out. Sooner or later I was going to kill the Executioner and his men."

"But you didn't kill him before he told us about the Dodo location," I argue.

"That's because I needed to find the whereabouts of the March Hare, save him and then get you with him and children on the plane and go finish my work. I knew he was behind this from the beginning."

"How is that possible?"

"The March Hare extracted all kinds of drugs and cures from plants in Wonderland. It was him who extracted the Lullaby, which helped Lewis Carroll with his migraines. No one but him could have cooked it."

"Frankly, I don't know what to say to you," I say. "I mean, you do all the worst things in the world. You lie, cheat, manipulate, but then somewhere between the lines you have a good cause. I am so confused."

"Don't be," Fabiola says. "Whatever cause he had, he risked the end of the world by taking you along. What if something had happened to you while you were there?"

It's a plausible thought, but it depends on whether ridding the world of the Executioner was as important as saving lives.

"So do you have any idea how I can kill Carolus?" I tell the Pillar, hoping he'll tell the truth this time.

"I don't know," he says. "I think your best bet is that the March remembers all the details of what happened with Carolus. I believe the solution lies in the Hare's ears – it'd be a shame having them stick out all the time for nothing."

"We'll take it from here," Fabiola says. "Now get out of here, Pillar."

The Pillar nods. He looks defeated in a way. Like I noticed before, he can hardly stand up to Fabiola. We all watch him walk out the door, wondering if we'll ever see him again—or if we ever want to see him again.

"And please stay away from Alice." Fabiola stabs the words in his back. I know if there's one thing he likes the most, it's to be near me. "Once the Inklings are set to go, we won't need you."

The Pillar slowly turns back. "Why do you hate me so much, White Queen?" he says. "I lost this for you." He waves his right hand in the air and points at something.

I blink, trying to interpret what he means. Lost what for her, Pillar? What in the church was he pointing at? Was he pointing at God? Has he lost his faith to her? It doesn't make sense.

Fabiola stiffens. The Pillar's words cut through her somehow. She fights the tears and stands straight, saying nothing.

"Get out, Pillar." She kills him now—and me. "Go pay the Queen of Hearts with the key in exchange for your revenge. Go spill blood and spread mayhem wherever you want, but not near us."

The Pillar turns around and walks out. As he does, he stops near one of the uninfected and scares her. "Boo!"

Chapter 89

Radcliffe asylum, Oxford

The Cheshire, in Todd's body now, grinned at his sister.

"You look awkward," she retorted. "Go find Dad and make fun of him."

"So you're not Tweedledee?" the Cheshire said.

"What? You've read those Alice in Wonderland books now? Aren't you too old for that?"

"No one's too old for those books, don't you think?" the Cheshire said. "So you're not Tweedledum, either?"

"I'm not," she says. "What's wrong with you today?"

"I guess it's the Alice in Wonderland books." The Cheshire cocked his head.

"You know what happened to me the first time my teacher read the book to us in class when I was younger?"

"No. What happened?"

"She kept reading it to the class, so fascinated by it," she said. "And I was like eleven or so. I couldn't fathom the books. My mind was reeling, truly."

"And then what happened?"

"I raised my hand after she finished and said, 'Teacher, is this

Lewis Carroll mad, or is he mad?'"

The Cheshire laughed aloud.

"My teacher was *mad* at me when I said that and spent the rest of the day explaining how this book was the pinnacle of literature and that the author was never mad and never took any drugs."

"And we all know what that means, of course."

"That he was mad and took drugs." She snickered.

"You know what's madder? That we love this book so much."

"I guess we're mad too," Tania said.

"We're all mad here." The Cheshire grinned.

"Oh, my God, Todd," Tania said. "Do that again."

"What? *We're all mad here?*"

"That's bombastically amazing. You look just like the Cheshire."

"Oh, come on. Who could match the Cheshire's creepy grin in that Disney movie?"

"No, seriously. Yours is even better," Tania said. "Please do it again."

"You know what I can do better? I can make my head disappear, too."

"Haha. Don't get carried away."

The Cheshire grinned. "Wanna see? Look."

But of course his head didn't disappear, because sometimes he was still bound by the body of the one he possessed. It seemed that not only was Todd not one of the Tweedles, but he also wasn't a good sport. His head wouldn't budge.

"You made me laugh, anyway," Tania said. "You should do that grin a lot. I think girls will like it. Girls like all kinds of weirds things, trust me."

"Are you having fun, children?" Dr. Truckle entered the cell.

"Lotsa fun and grins." The Cheshire put his hands around his father's arm in hopes of possessing the man's body to find his way out of the asylum.

To his surprise, he couldn't get into Tom's body.

The Cheshire, still trapped inside the teenager, stared suspiciously at Dr. Tom Truckle. To his knowledge, it was only Wonderlanders he could not possess. *Who are you, Dr. Truckle?*

Chapter 90

St Peter's, The Vatican

"I think you were a bit harsh on the Pillar." I tell Fabiola.

She dismisses my comment and checks on the March Hare in the confession booth. "Did you remember anything of importance yet?"

"Nothing, White Queen," he replied. "But I feel the drug wearing off. I should remember all that happened soon enough."

"Then you have no choice but to go to Geneva," Fabiola tells me. "Take your umbrella. I have a feeling it's the way to kill Carolus."

"It makes sense. If Lewis gave it to me, then maybe it's the weapon to kill his darker half with." I stare at the laughable umbrella that has saved my life repeatedly.

Fabiola's phone rings. "Go check if the plane is ready. I need to answer this."

I don't go out but call the chauffeur who's outside somewhere. He landed the chopper on top of a locked building, so he wouldn't bump into citizens looking for a fight.

"All set," the chauffeur says. "Come over. We'll be in Geneva soon enough."

I hang up and tell the White Queen, but she shocks me with the latest news.

"I know what the Queen is up to."

"I'm so curious about your sources inside the Queen's castle," I say. "What is it?"

"You know the Geneva meeting will have the world's most prestigious presidents, right?"

"Sure."

"It will have the president of United States meet the Queen of England. The Israeli presidents meet the most prestigious Arab president. The Russian president meet the Ukrainian president and so forth, to name a few."

"Those presidents' nations are in continuous conflict with each other," Fabiola says. "Usually, in every world meeting of this kind, they settle for courtesy and etiquette, choose not to clash against one another or say what's really on their mind."

"I'm not following."

"Most of the world's leaders hate each other, Alice. Their countries hate the others' countries too." Fabiola holds me by the arms. "Everyone in the world knows that. But we always find a way to make peace in the world. You know how?"

"I get it now," I say. "By not saying the truth."

"That's why the Queen took Carolus with her. He has some of the plague's scent left. She is going to pour it into their tea at the meeting. And you know what will happen then?"

"Every president will tell the truth," I say absently.

"The bad truth none of us can handle."

"And then the world will be in continuous wars, nations against nations. It's what the Queen loves most."

"How is this different from a plague?"

"Alice. What happened to you?" Fabiola says. "In a plague everyone dies. Poor, rich, powerful, weak, buyer, seller. In a war, a lot of people get rich. You sell weapons, give the illusion of safety to those you protect. It's a different ball game."

I am not quite sure I really understand the difference, but I know the Queen needs to be stopped first, even before killing Carolus. Maybe the two things have to be done at once.

"This is a bit too much for me." I shrug.

"I know," Fabiola says. "That's why I'm coming with you to Geneva."

Chapter 91

On the way to Geneva

The Cheshire, disguised in another cell mate, sat next to Tom Truckle in the plane going to Geneva.

He'd persuaded him he knew how to get in, and that Tom needed to be there since the world's presidents would discuss the consequences of the plague, something Tom was interested in.

The Cheshire had to do it, because as much as he was looking for the Tweedles, he was incredibly curious about Dr. Truckle's identity.

"Are you sure we can get in?" Tom asked, looking at the world below.

"I'm sure. I've always had my secret ways to get into the Queen's meetings."

"Well, I sure hope so. I've always suspected that the world's elite people had planned a way out of the apocalypse, like a ship in the sea, or even escaping to the moon. I read about it."

"Of course. I'm as curious as you are. Let's hope we expose their plans."

"But you never told me why you admitted yourself to the asylum, Jack." Dr. Truckle said. "I always thought you weren't mad."

"I have my reasons."

"I think you're in love with that bonkers girl, Alice." He elbowed him. "What's with that girl? Why is everyone so interested in her?"

"She is special." The Cheshire grinned. Possessing Jack's body didn't fall under the rule that he couldn't enter a Wonderlander's body. Because let's face it. Jack wasn't a Wonderlander anymore. He was dead. A figment of his own imagination.

Which rather irritated the Cheshire. How could he possess a nobody's body? It was mindboggling, even for a cat.

Chapter 92

Geneva, Switzerland

Margaret watched the Queen rub her hands with enthusiasm.

Soon the presidents would all enter the main hall and have their conference. The first part was planned to be aired for the public— well, the few channels that hadn't been brought down by the angry public yet. The second part was going to be a closed meeting where they'd arrange the escape of the richest people in case the plague had no cure.

The Queen's made sure there wasn't going to be a second part of the meeting.

She'd injected the tea with the truth serum already, and even called it the Tea to Truth. "Oh, the Mad Hatter would've loved this if he were here. The real Mad Hatter, I mean."

"I still don't understand trying to make the world's most powerful presidents clash against each other when the world is going to end anyway," Margaret had to say.

"I know what I am doing. Didn't I say don't question me? Besides, villains always do it in James Bond movies." She stood on a high chair, checking out her beauty in a mirror. "Do you think I look good for the end of the world?"

"If you're planning to take a photo with you to the afterlife," Margaret mumbled.

"I heard you," the Queen said. "Don't you think I'm not planning to conquer the afterlife after I conquer the world, ugly duchess."

Margaret shrugged, having no idea what to do. She had already been angry enough, hearing what the Pillar did to her investments in Columbia, but this wasn't the right time to teach this hookah man a lesson. She needed to deal with this crazy Queen first. What did she know that Margaret didn't?

It must have all happened in her conversation with Carolus. If the Queen's guards would only let her meet with this man.

"I'm ready," the Queen chirped. "Now, did you call Fabiola?"

"Yes. She didn't recognize my voice. I told her I was a rebelling guard from Buckingham Palace who wished the Queen's reign would end," Margaret said. "I told her that you are taking Carolus to Geneva, and that she and Alice have to come and save the world by killing Carolus."

"Fantastic. I bet she took the bait."

"Like a starving fish," Margaret said. "She is coming here in a while."

"Great. That's the deal between me and Carolus. He gave me what was left of the plague so I could put in the tea in exchange for handing him this Alice girl."

"I thought he wanted the Lullaby pill."

"He needed the pill when he had migraines. I gave him one to ease his pain, but his real plan was to lure Alice. He first asked me for the Pillar, because he knew that the easiest way to find Alice was through the Pillar, but I told him I have faster and easier ways to get her."

"So this whole plague was to help him find Alice?"

"Some loon, right?" The Queen grinned. "He said he wasn't sure who the Real Alice was. That the only way he'd find her is to threaten the world's safety."

"I'm not following, My Queen."

"Think about it. The Real Alice will always stand up to save the world like we were told in that prophecy. Apparently, Carolus believes in it."

"Strange way to find the Real Alice, but he has a point. Still, why does he wants to meet her so bad?"

"Maybe he wants to kill her, but don't ask me why. All that matters is that I get the world's presidents into a war. And it's always good to get rid of any girl named Alice, in case she is the real one." She rolled her eyes.

Margaret watched the Queen enter the meeting hall. She thought it was a good idea she'd also told Fabiola the Queen's plan. Now maybe this annoying Alice would find a heroic way to stop the Queen from her executing her plan, and then she would die in Carolus's hands.

Now that's what they called two birds with one stone.

Chapter 93

Pillar's Chopper on its way to Geneva

Fabiola changes into modern clothes inside the plane.

She comes to show her formal, businesswoman dress. And she looks rather shy, or confused.

"You look good," I say. And she does. I don't think she realizes she has an athletic feminine-looking body. Or maybe it's me who just doesn't know who she was before she became a nun.

"I haven't changed my nun's dress in years." She's almost blushing. "It's a bit uncomfortable to me."

"You're always beautiful, White Queen," the March says, although he should be trying to remember the exact incident with Carolus.

"You are," I say.

"I don't want to look beautiful," she says. "I want to look convincing enough that we can get through the UN's building gates."

"Don't worry," the chauffeur says. "I've taken care of that. The Pillar sent me fake invitations for the three of you."

This doesn't warm Fabiola toward him though.

"I think, as much of a mystery as he is, he still tries to help," I say.

"You don't know him, Alice," she says. "He shouldn't have killed more people. You think he solved the world's drug problem?

Tomorrow, another Executioner will be born."

"I understand."

"This is exactly what I was talking about when I told about you staring darkness in the eyes, and not getting stained with it."

"I think I get it. I felt so much hate and anger in Columbia, I was about to go on a rampage, too."

"The Pillar never got it. That's why he isn't a good man. He wants to fight fire with fire, not admitting that he likes it."

"I have to say he does like it." I stretch my arms. "But forget about him. You know what I like about this moment?"

"What?"

"The three of us are on a mission together. Three more and the Inklings will be complete."

"I'm an Inklings' member?" The March giggles. "So frabjous."

"You know what would be frabjous?" I tell him. "If you remembered any useful details about the plague. Maybe there is a cure, after all."

"I'm trying my best." His ears dangle a bit. "Believe me, I do. I've even looked through all my pockets for a clue, but..."

Suddenly his ears stand erect again. His eyes bulge out like usual.

"What is it?" Fabiola says.

"I found something in my jacket's pocket. It's a hidden pocket I totally forgot about."

"And what did you find in there?" I say.

The March says nothing. He elevates his hands, showing four thin tubes, like the ones you use in a chemistry lab.

"What are those?" I inquire.

"I still need to remember that, but..." His eyes dart between me and Fabiola. "I think this could be the cure."

Chapter 94

Geneva, Switzerland

"**W**here is Alice?" Carolus' face twitched.

"Calm down," the Queen told him, not facing him but the presidents of the world from behind the curtain overlooking the huge meeting room. "She is on her way. Besides, didn't I give you a Lullaby pill?"

"It was just one pill. Not enough."

"Well, then save your anger for Alice when she arrives. I have no idea why everyone is so interested in this girl."

"Because she is the Real Alice."

"And how do you know that?"

"Who else would walk around trying to save the world?" Carolus said. "It must be her."

"That's the Pillar's doing. He wants something from her, probably the whereabouts of the keys. That's all. She isn't Alice."

"She must be." Carolus' head ached. His jaw looked tense.

"I think you should wait in the other room for her to arrive," the Queen said. "You can't show up in the meeting anyway. Everyone knows you're the madman with the hookahs."

"Not even when Alice arrives?"

"You can do whatever you want to her when she comes, but not in the meeting room. I need the press to document and videotape the presidents swearing and humiliating each other when the tea's effect begins. Wait for her when she leaves the room. I'll get my guards to help you catch her."

"I don't need your guards. You don't know what my plan is."

"I surely don't." The Queen rolled her eyes. Lewis's split persona had always been cuckoo in the head. "And I don't want to. All I care about is seeing the presidents clash against one another."

"Good luck with that." Carolus turned around.

"Wait," the Queen said. "I just need to make sure we understand each other, that what you told me about the plague is true, or my plan will be useless."

"I told you the truth."

"'The 'truth' is not the best word to use on this occasion."

"Rest assured. What I told you about the plague is a fact. You go rule the world while I get Alice."

"Agreed." The Queen rubbed her hands and entered the meeting.

Once she got inside, a butler offered her tea.

"I don't need tea," she mumbled, sitting down. "Do I look like I need to tell the truth?"

The butler, who was Indian, walked away confused, cursing those arrogant English people who'd wrongfully occupied his land for years. He suddenly realized how much he despised them.

The Queen of Hearts smiled, listening to his mumbling. Good. The Tea of Truth was working.

Chapter 95

Geneva, Switzerland

"**Y**ou need to remember," I tell the March while inside the special limousine the Pillar rented for us. "Are those tubes the cure?"

"First of all, they aren't just tubes. They are syringes inside." He examines them in his hands. "But I think they are."

"Think isn't good enough," Fabiola says.

The limousine crosses the gate and we're parking next to the most important presidents in the world. I watch each one of them get out of his car, surrounded by the bulkiest guards. It's ironic to see this kind of luxury and protection while the world is withering away everywhere else.

"If everyone is a president around here, who are we?" Fabiola asks the chauffeur.

"You're Queen and Princess of Bonkerstan," he announces, handing over our fake passports.

"That's not a country." I comment.

"That's not even a real word" The March chuckles. "Oh, I'm the Minister of Cuckoology. Love that."

"You know how many countries exist with such weird names?" the chauffeur says. "The world is too big, and the weirder the country's name, the more no one cares. Just flash your passport on the way in. Act like a queen and princess. If asked, tell them you have a cure for the plague and show them the syringes. You need to get inside and stop the presidents from drinking the Queen's tea."

"So I didn't need to dress like a business woman," Fabiola says. "I'm a queen, after all."

We step out of the limo, and we're the only ones without protection or guards. I see Fabiola hide her Vorpal sword inside her dress and raise an eyebrow at her.

"In case your umbrella isn't good enough," she says.

"Time to kick some butt," the March Hare says.

We both shoot him a straight look. He shouldn't be joking. He should remember things.

We wave at the other presidents on the way in. Most of them stare at us from head to toe, wondering how it's possible we're here.

"Bonkerstan!" I celebrate, waving my umbrella.

Suddenly, all kinds of reporters surround us.

"Are you here to save the world? "A woman sticks her mic into my face.

"Of course," I say. "Me and my mother." I point at Fabiola.

"You speak English?" the reporter wonders. "Could you please tell us where Bonkerstan is on the map?"

"It's not on the map." I am improvising. "We asked it not to be included."

"We need to protect our resources." Fabiola catches up.

"Really?" another reporter asks. "What kind of resources?"

"It's hard to explain," I begin to stutter. What did I get myself into? "It's more of…"

"Jub jubs." Fabiola saves me again. "We produce about fourteen million jub jubs a year."

"What's a jub jub—"

"I think it's more like thirteen million." Now I cut in.

"Of course." Fabiola distracts the reporter until we get into the building. "Considering the last million was all infested with marshmallows."

"I'm sorry," the reporter tenses. "But who are you, really?"

Fabiola and I say nothing. We're only a few meters into the building, and this reporter could expose us.

"We are the one who have the cure!" the March steps in. The he turns to me and Fabiola. "I mean it. I found a note in my pocket. It says all we have to do is inject the infected with this syringe."

"Then what are waiting for?" I pull out one of the syringes and dart into the building. Fabiola and the March follow me. All the reporters are commenting on how *bonkers* we are.

Chapter 96

"Sit here," the Cheshire told Tom Truckle. "It's a bit far from the presidential area, but we'll be able to see and hear everything."

"Thank you, Jack. I didn't think you'd be so useful."

"I didn't think I'd be either." The Cheshire took in a long breath. It was good being in Jack's body. Young, healthy, and feeling so alive. Why hadn't he done that long ago? Something told him he'd stay in the boy's body for a long time. Maybe it was time to forget about the Cheshire and just be Jack.

He enjoyed how most of the girls giggled at him. Jack was attractive and athletic. All the Cheshire needed was to learn how to act like Jack.

"Oh, tea," the Cheshire said, taking what the butler was offering. "My father used to love his five o'clock milk—I mean tea, of course."

"Did he love flying saucers too?" Tom said, squinting at something in the distance."

"No, we cats—I mean, my father never believed in extraterrestrials."

"I'm not talking about that. I am talking about teacups and flying saucers." Tom was pointing at saucers flying their way now.

"Duck, Dr. Truckle!" The Cheshire pulled him under the stairs with him.

Teacups and saucers and vases were flying and crashing against the walls everywhere, accompanied by presidents swearing and shouting at each other.

"What is going on?" Tom wailed.

"Nothing much," the Cheshire said. "World War Wonderland—I mean World War III."

Chapter 97

UN Headquarters, Geneva, Switzerland

We're too late. The hall is a teacups and saucers festival.

The most surprised of us is the March Hare, staring at the presidents of the world swearing and throwing teacups at each other.

And the worst part is that it's all being caught on TV.

"Each one has his own war," Fabiola says. "The Arabs and Jews throwing all kinds of china at each other."

"My God," I say. "The words they say to each other. Humiliating."

"It's a centuries old conflict," Fabiola says. "And it seems all this peace talk was nothing but a front. The Tea of Truth proves that."

"North Korea and South Korea, too." The March points at them in the far corner.

"Is that the Russian and Ukrainian presidents?" I point.

"Not sure," Fabiola says. "But I'm sure that's the American president throwing china at the Queen of Hearts."

"She is enjoying this," the March says.

We watch her atop a high chair raiding the American ambassadors with her favorite teacups.

"The Queen shoots teacups better than Tiger Woods on a golf course," a voice says behind us.

A voice we all know well. The Pillar.

"I thought I told you..." Fabiola begins.

The Pillar pulls her down instantly. A series of teacups swoosh above her head and knocked a reporter down to the floor. Fabiola looks more annoyed he saved her this time. She waves his hand off and looks the other way.

"Is she always that way?" the Pillar tells me. "I thought nuns had manners."

"We don't have time for this." I tuck a syringe against his chest. "Dip this into the American president's neck."

"I'm going to kill him?"

"No. It will cure him of the plague. Sadly, we only have four. So our best shot is to save the American president, Iranian, Israeli and Egyptian."

"I'd say the China and German presidents are good ones, too," Fabiola says. "We're not sure if offending the Germans won't give birth to another Hitler."

"Basically the most powerful president." I duck as another saucer almost knocks me down. "The aim is to cool the world down and stop them from the telling the truth about how they feel about each other."

"You want one in your chest too, Fabiola?" the Pillar says.

She dismisses him and turns toward the presidents. "I'll take the Jews' and Arabs'."

"You should take the American president," I tell the Pillar.

"Why me?"

"Just do as I say," I demand. "I'll make sure you're doing well and then go look for Carolus."

"Ah, I forgot. First make sure World War III won't happen, and then make sure to save the lazy human who's done nothing to find a cure."

"That's it." I'm not going to argue now.

"I think you will need to stay longer, Alice." The March grits his teeth against all things crashing around us.

"Why?"

"You need to inject the Queen of Hearts."

"She is a Wonderlander. She can't get infected with the truth."

"Not if it's inhaled from the Hookah of Hearts, but she injected it into the tea, and that's a different story. I just remembered."

"Well, you should have remembered about two years ago," the Pillar says. "No wonder she is all bonkers, shooting saucers like a short stocky alien in a movie I never saw."

"All right." I grit my teeth. "So I'll inject the Queen."

"Did you notice we've been discussing this a bit too long?" Fabiola urges us. "Let's get going."

"But they always have long chats in movies when bullets are showering all around them." The Pillar has one of those childish episodes again.

"Stop it," I shush him. "Let's go. In the chest, remember?"

"Wait," the March itches his ears. "I just remembered something now."

The Pillar rolls his eyes.

"The syringes don't work when you pinch them into the chest," the March says. "It has to be the..."

"The what?" I am as impatient as the Pillar now.

"In the butt."

Fabiola and I are so shocked we can't utter a word. But the Pillar curves an eyebrow and has a smile on his face. "Fantabulous. Why didn't you say so from the beginning?"

Chapter 98

Parking Lot, UN Headquarters, Geneva, Switzerland

Carolus was close to hitting his head against the walls. It hurt so much. He needed another Lullaby pill. Why hadn't this terrible Queen given him more than one pill?

"Cool down," he spoke to himself. "It'll only be moments before Alice comes looking for you outside. Be patient."

But he couldn't. He fell on his knees, his head buried in his hands. "I hate you, Lewis Carroll!"

While on the asphalt floor outside the meeting hall, he heard a voice in his head. A voice so evil he could not dismiss it.

Stand up. You're close to achieving what no one has in years. You're so close.

"Yes, my master." Carolus propped himself on one knee, the pain surging into his spine now.

The voice continued.

The plan with the plague has been brilliant. Two years we have waited for this to happen. We had to bring wrath onto the world to get the attention of one girl.

"Of course, master," Carolus said. "I must not give up. It'll only be minutes until she comes out and the plan is complete." Slowly, he began to rise to his feet, a dark grin forming on his face. "I'm sure this plan will be taught in history books. It's the plan of the century."

Chapter 99

UN Headquarters, Geneva, Switzerland

Watching Fabiola swoosh her Vorpal sword at whoever tries to stop us is both maddening and fascinating.

The best part is how good she is. She fights like an expert samurai, and it makes me more curious about her past. I watch her curve behind a few presidents and stab the first with the syringe, not emptying all of it so she can still save a few others.

The German ambassador looks so relived after his injection, as if he's just been to the bathroom.

"Just the butt, or do we have to pull down the pants?" the Pillar says, dodging punches from a bodyguard who seems to want to hit anyone he comes across.

"Just do it!" I jump on top of a table and kick a few guards in the face with the back of my umbrella.

A lost tea cup knocks me down a moment after. I summersault back on the floor. A few None Fu techniques come in handy now.

"Bravo, Alice!" The March claps his hands, a fraction of a second before a huge pie slams into him. He starts licking at it.

I watch the Pillar inject the Iranian president in the butt and suppress a laugh. If only I could take a snapshot of that moment. It looks hilarious. The Pillar looks embarrassed that he did it. But the consequences are amazing. A smile on the president's face, trying to calm everyone down and listening to the sound of reason.

However, there is this reporter from outside still tailing me. "Didn't you say Bonkerstan has a cure?"

No time to explain now. I sprint on top of the tables and reach for the Queen of Hearts. If I could only get my hands on her, I'd inject her right away.

But she rewards me with a back hand like a professional tennis player. I stagger back, birds twittering around me.

On the floor, I see the Pillar trying to get hold of the American president. But it seems the president is fixated on throwing saucers at the Queen of Hearts. I wonder how this will look like in tomorrow's headlines.

They're so close. It'll only be seconds before this fight turns physical.

The TV is broadcasting.

"I'm close to getting him, Alice," the Pillar says. "You close in on the Queen from the back, and we'll do'em both in one move."

The TV reporter tailing me doesn't like the sound of that at all.

I prop myself up and jump on the Queen, knocking her to the ground. The broadcasting crew is already shocked by my move—as if none of what's going on around them is shocking.

I look as if I'm strangling the Queen, who only chirps one sentence, *off with her head!*

Once I get hold of her, I realize the Pillar is gripping the American president as well.

"Time to save the world." The Pillar snickers, bending the president over as if he is going to punish him for being bad by slapping his butt.

Saying it looks surreal is an understatement. I can't believe this is happening.

In one move, the Pillar and I inject the American president and the Queen of England with the syringes in their butts with grins of victory on our faces.

"Yes!" the Pillar says.

Turning my head, the reporter tailing me is dangling her tongue like a Mushroomer. Behind her, the camera crew have this unexplainable expression on their faces. They don't know whether to laugh hysterically or cry.

Chapter 100

"Is that Alice sticking her hands in the Queen's...?" Tom Truckle stood speechless staring at them.

"It's your fault if you ask me." The Cheshire, still posing as Jack, cops a laugh. "You're the one who let her out of the asylum."

"But even if she is the craziest of the crazy, why would she do that?" Of course Tom knew this wasn't the Queen of England but the Queen of Hearts. He'd thought that last week's events at the Event were the craziest he'd ever experience, but this topped that a million times. "I really could use my pills now."

"I see you gulp a lot of those," the Cheshire commented. "Are they good?"

"I don't even know. I just take them to stay sane in this world gone mad."

"Do they have a name? I could buy me some."

"You won't find them anywhere. They're called Lullaby."

Chapter 101

Parking Lot, UN Headquarters, Geneva, Switzerland

I leave the meeting hall looking for Carolus.

There is no need to stay in. Most of the presidents have been cured and are apologizing for what happened, talking world peace now—and of course what to do with the real plague that's threatening the world.

I also left Fabiola trying to see if the March can cook more of this cure, although it'd be impossible to inject the whole population in their butts to save their lives.

Just a few feet out of the meeting hall, Carolus Ludovicus grins at me, although he still looks to be in pain.

"I was waiting for you," he says.

"For me?" I am confused. Why would someone who I need to kill wait for me? But I have nothing to do but talk now. The sun behind me sets low, and I haven't figured out how to kill him yet so I can save the world.

"I've been waiting for you for years, Alice."

"Years?" I'm more and more confused.

"Since the first day I materialized into life. You have no idea how many headaches I had to give Lewis until he was weak enough to let me out into the world."

"It's a pretty hard concept to grasp, that you're his darker side, I mean."

"The Cheshire likes to say 'we're all mad here.'" He's half circling me from a distance, his head tilted to the right a bit. "He is wrong. 'We're all schizophrenic here' is the right phrase. Lewis is no different front the rest of us. Darkness lurks in all of us."

"Don't compliment yourself." I'm still buying time. "You're just a figment of your imagination."

"Isn't Jack the same?" His stare is piercing through me. "But you love Jack and don't love me."

"Don't compare yourself to Jack. What do you really want?"

"I want what you want."

"I don't think so." I slowly step closer to him. Maybe I need to lock him up somewhere until I figure out how to kill him. "You want to laugh at the world by showing them that they can't handle the truth."

"And isn't it fun?"

"No it isn't. If you want fun, go ride a roller coaster. Now, what do you really want? Why aren't you running away from me when you know I'm the only who can kill Carroll's split persona?"

"Why do you think I'm not running, Alice?" He dares me and slowly limps toward me.

This is strange. I don't understand what's going on.

"You think I made the March Hare cook this plague to end the world?"

"It's a plausible assumption." I'm not going to stop. I try not to be scared of him. It's like playing tip-top, only waiting to see who will kill the other first.

"And why would I want to end the world?" He flaps his eyes sideways, and balloons start falling from the sky.

This is surreal. I never thought balloons could scare me this much.

"So explain it to me. You plague the world but still don't want anyone to die. Either I'm mad or it's you whose screws are loose."

"None of us are mad, Alice." Closer. "I created this plague for one reason—other than having fun by laughing at humans killing each other because of the truth, of course."

"I have an asylum I have to go back to, so cut it short because I don't have all night. Sleeping early is good for mad girls like me."

"You want short? Okay." He stops, his cheeks twitching against the pain. Maybe I don't have to kill him at all. Maybe the migraine will. "I created this plague to find you."

"You wanted to see me? Why not send an SMS?" I keep approaching.

"Because how do I know you're the real Alice?"

Now I stop.

"I had to create an end of the world scenario because only the Real Alice would stand up to face me," he says. "If you weren't the Real Alice, you wouldn't be standing here this very moment."

There is a lump in my throat. "And why did you want to find me?"

Chapter 102

UN Headquarters, Geneva, Switzerland

Fabiola finally escaped the guards who caught her, thinking she was a terrorist. Funny how mad people think of you as mad once you cure them.

"Where is Alice?" She bumped into the Pillar.

"Outside. She'll kill Carolus to stop the plague."

"Something's not right, Pillar. You have to save her. I mean save him." She hit the Pillar in the chest.

"I don't understand."

"The March Hare just remembered why Carolus imprisoned him in Brazil."

"Why?"

"Because he feared the March would remember his plan and expose him."

"His plan? You mean the plague?"

"No, the real plan behind the plague."

"You mean Carolus doesn't want to end the world?"

"No. He wanted the plague to lead him to the real Alice. It was a test so he could find her."

"Find her?" The Pillar thought for a moment. "Find her and what?

Kill her?"

"That's a possibility, but I don't think that's it." She was trying to frantically find an exit, as the guards had locked them for security.

"Then why did he use the plague to lead him to Alice?"

"Don't you get it?"

The Pillar's face drooped as if he'd just aged twenty years. "Lewis Carroll!"

Chapter 103

"I had to find you so I could finally kill you, Alice Wonder."

I am about to laugh at him. "That's not even my real name."

"You're right," he says. "I needed to kill you with my own hands, Mary Ann."

He begins approaching again, his balloon showing the night all around me. I wonder if they are some kind of weapon. He sounds so confident.

"Back off." I point my umbrella at him. "Or I'll shoot."

"You know the Bandersnatch bullets won't kill me."

The worst thing is that I do know. What could possibly kill Carolus?

"I thought Lewis told you how to kill me." He stopped again. Carolus surely likes to chat a lot.

"Everyone keeps telling me Lewis must have told." I am going crazy. "But he hasn't."

"Maybe he did, and you just missed the message."

"No! He didn't." I take a deep breath after losing control for a moment. "He showed me to his studio. I saw one of the doors to Wonderland. I saw the rabbit in his pocket. I saw the photographs of the girls he took. He talked to me, and he was nice to me." I realize tears are about to trickle down my cheeks. I can't help it. "He never even told me about you."

"That's because I am the part he likes to forget the most," Carolus says. "Like everyone else, no one wants to admit their dark half exists."

"You sure do talk too much." I hold back the tears. "What do you really want? You would have killed me already if that's what you planned all this for."

"I like a fair fight," His shoulders twitch now. "It th-th-thrills me."

This is when I realize the full beast is facing me now.

"How fair can this get? I don't remember how to kill you."

"So-so let me remind you." The grin on his face could kill a few people in this life alone.

"Tell me." I am reluctant, but if he wants to play, let's play.

"Lewis must have given you something precious and told you not to tell about it."

"He did," Sorry, Lewis. A lot of people know about the key. It's too late to pretend I don't have it. "A key."

"Never realized what it's for?"

"No."

"How about you check that small button on your umbrella weapon for a start?"

"Button?" I look and find it instantly. I remember pushing it before. It opens a small groove where a bullet should fit in, except no bullet ever did.

"Now try to load your umbrella with the key."

My heart races. I pull out the key, about to fit it in.

"Not all keys open doors, Alice," Carolus says. "Some keys open skulls."

Chapter 104

It's hard to tell how long it takes to squeeze the key bullet into place.

At first, my shaking hands drop it. Then, as I kneel to pick it up, it suddenly rains, not balloons, but icy waters.

With a blurry vision, on my knees, I feel the earth, looking for my lost key, well aware of Carolus running my direction.

Faster, Alice. Don't think about him coming at you. Just do what you have to do. A fraction of a second could save lives.

I find the key, not looking in the monster's direction, tuck it in as I'm standing to my feet. I grip the umbrella with a fist of steel, close one eye to aim better, and...

"Stop!" The Pillar grips my umbrella.

I'm still gripping it too, and I won't let go. What's with the Pillar? But what really stops me from shooting Carolus is that he stops once he lays his eyes on the Pillar.

"It's a trick," the Pillar says behind me. "Don't shoot him."

"What do you mean? Killing him is the only way to save the world."

"No. It's also the only way to kill Lewis Carroll for good."

This throws me off. What did he just say?

"Carolus infected the world to find you, not because only the Real Alice will be brave enough to confront him, but because only the Real

Alice will have Lewis Carroll's most precious key."

Carolus is slowly getting madder now. "Don't believe him. The Pillar is a liar. Always has been."

"I'm not lying, Alice." The Pillar's voice is stable, smooth, nothing rocks him away. "Didn't you ever ask yourself why Lewis didn't remind you of the whereabouts of the rest of the keys when he gave you this one in the Tom Tower?"

"It crossed my mind, but I never understood." I'm still aiming at Carolus.

"Because he doesn't know. Lewis only has one key in his possession. A special key. One that opens skulls, like Carolus said. Lewis gave you the key, the bullet, that kills him."

"Why?"

"In case he couldn't defeat his split persona, Carolus Ludovicus, his inner demon," the Pillar says. "Lewis Carroll trapped all Wonderland Monster, except of one. His darker part which he couldn't tame or control. Killing this part kills Lewis. True, they are like night and day, darkness and light, but they are one."

"You were ready to die so you could kill Lewis?" I stare at Carolus.

"I hate him!" Carolus drops to his knees. "All these migraines. All this pain he went through and he still loves those terrible kids. He still writes those stupid books and poems to make people laugh. I hated how he still had passion for life after all that he'd been through – both of us have been through. I wanted him to unleash his anger on the world after the Circus. Why does he still love human children after the Circus? I never understood. Why he lives with his pain, not telling anyone about it. It drives me crazy. Lewis Carroll must die."

I'm shattering on the inside. It's not the icy rain. And not even the exhaustion I feel. It's the darkness I see inside Carolus Ludovicus. How come this kind of hatred exists in the first place? "I still have to kill him," I tell the Pillar.

"Why?"

"Look at him. I won't let a monster like him run away. He will run away like the Cheshire. I am not going to let the villains escape every time. And the plague. If I don't kill him the people in the world will kill each other."

"Saving the world might not be like in the movies, Alice," the Pillar says. "It's not really about killing the villain right away. It's about saving lives first. We'll figure out how to face the plague on our own."

"No." I cement my feet and make sure I have a clear shot of Carolus. "This kind of darkness in the world has to end."

"Remember when you told me Fabiola told you about staring darkness in the eyes?" The Pillar's voice is unusually soft. "Don't let it stain you, Alice. Don't let bad people turn you into an equally violent hero." He hesitates then says, "Don't be like me."

Chapter 105

Carolus disappears in the rain, behind his floating balloons, just like the darker side in all of us. The Pillar says it's better this way. That there is nothing wrong with having a dark side. It helps us know, and appreciate, our better side.

It's hard to take moral advice from a serial killer, but Fabiola tells me the same when she arrives. It takes her a whole minute to pull my finger free of the trigger.

Hypnotized by this strange world, they show me back to the Pillar's new plane. I get on. Fabiola makes me a cup of warm milk. The Pillar jokes that it reminds him of the man we met in Mushroomland who thought he was a bottle of milk.

His joke doesn't resonate with me. I just let a monster go. The world is so dark right now I'd really like to sleep.

Some time later, we land in the Vatican. Fabiola brushes a kiss on my forehead. "At least you now know you're the Real Alice."

Then she disappears out of the plane. It occurs to me that the world sounds too quiet outside, but I'm too tired.

I fall asleep again.

The next time I wake up I'm in my cell back in the asylum. They've bought me a new bed. It's clean. Comfy. I am thinking it's too late for such luxury. The world will end in a few hours.

Next time I wake, the Pillar hands me that bottle of milk again.

"I'm not the Cheshire, don't worry." He jokes. "Drink it. You'll be good tomorrow."

"Wait. I thought there was no tomorrow?"

"I guess you didn't hear it while you were asleep." He stops on his way out. "The March remembered what happened exactly. It turns out Carolus instructed him to design a plague that would wear off in three days."

"Impossible."

"It's true. Of course the world is left a bit damaged. A few million divorces, coworkers who never want to see each other again, and a few thousand dead. The same you read in everyday news. But we're still alive."

I try to smile, but my lips feel as rigid and fragile as china. I'm afraid if I laugh I'll break in two.

"And nothing is impossible by the way," the Pillar says before leaving. "Only losing hope is possible."

Chapter 106

The Pillar's Cell, Radcliffe Asylum, Oxford
A few days later

I am slowly tiptoeing my way up to the Pillar's cell. There is hardly anyone blocking my way. I'm suspicious.

When I arrive, there are many Mushroomers lined up next to the Pillar's cell. They're craning their heads up, watching the news on the Pillar's private TV.

Closer, I see Tom Truckle, and two teenagers beside him, sharing the Mushroomers' stare at whatever is being broadcasted.

"Alice!" the Pillar chirps from his couch, a hookah hose tucked between his lips. "Come watch this."

I walk among the Mushroomers. They all look happy I am better now. Even Tom makes way for me to step up into the Pillar's cell.

"We're wanted criminals, me and you, isn't this amazing?" The Pillar points at the TV.

I read the headlines: A serial killer and his daughter invaded the UN's headquarters yesterday, along with a strange-looking old man, trying to invoke chaos. It's unclear whether they wanted to kill the American president or the Queen of England.

"It's strange no one's talking about the plague," I remark.

"The plague is one day old. That's too old for news channels." The Pillar drags on his hose, wiggling his feet. "But us trying to kill the president, that's news. They're discussing if they should send us to Guantanamo."

"We're that dangerous?"

"I had no idea," the Pillar says.

"I'm glad they didn't drag Fabiola into this."

"They can't." He waves his pipe. "Politics. It's like saying Jesus Christ came down and peed into the Queen's pot of nuts. Conflict of interest is what it's called. Keep looking. It gets better."

"Why are you so stoked about this?"

"Because I just saw it ten minutes ago. Just keep looking."

I watch the host receive a bulk of papers, read and make a face about it. She says, "Apparently, only two of the criminals will be sent to Guantanamo. The elder man, Professor Carter Pillar, must have been there by mistake."

"What?" I turn to him.

"Just keep watching. It's so frabjous I'm going to vomit butterflies."

The host continues. "Professor Pillar turned out to be a national hero, having ended the reign of drug cartels in Columbia on his own."

"You're a national hero?" I point accusingly at him.

"For only five minutes. Just keep looking."

"Okay." I look around. "Did you see Jack by the way?"

"He escaped. We don't know where he is. Don't worry. He always comes back. Now, look!"

This time the host has decided to change her mind again. "Sorry for this confusion, but the newest thing we know is that the three of them, Carter Pillar, Alice Wonder, and Jittery Jinks all escaped lunatic asylums during the plague which explains their mischievous behaviors, including the horrible matter of killing hundreds of innocent Columbian men."

"Told ya. Hero for five minutes," the Pillar says.

"This will only make my problems worse." Tom Truckle grunted. "I should have never let you two out of here."

I am speechless. It's a mad world indeed. But aside from needing some time to reflect on what happened with Carolus, I need to find Jack. Did he escape, looking for me?

"Where are you going?" The Pillar pulls me back. "You haven't seen the best part."

This time, when he points at the TV, a broad laugh from the heart escapes my lungs.

They're airing a still image of when the Pillar and I were injecting the Queen and the American president. From this angle, this picture looks so misleading. The Pillar looks as if he has his hands up the president's butt, mine in the Queen's.

And it's not just that. The grins of victory on our face proves without a doubt we're the looniest loons in the world.

The Pillar tries to suppress the laugh for a second but then explodes. He throws the hookah and pulls my hand and starts dancing with me.

Then the Mushroomers start laughing.

A few wardens snap out of the shock of what they're looking at and join us laughing hysterically.

Even Tom's teenagers laugh with us.

Everyone laughs but Tom, who pulls out a load of pills and swallows them without water. He then stiffens, unable to control the laughs. Trying to shout at us doesn't work. The veins on his neck stick out with anger, and I'm afraid he is going to have a heart attack.

Then a miracle happens.

Tom Truckle begins laughing like a madman. I don't think he knows what he is laughing about, but it's progress from him.

Chapter 107

"**G**et your hands off me!" The Queen roared at Margaret, trying to mend her wounds. "I have an itch as big as an apple on my butt."

"Royal butt heals faster than all" A young man enters her chamber all of a sudden.

The Queen and Margaret look perplexed.

"Don't worry, I'm not Jack," the Cheshire said. "I just borrowed him for a while. Very useful, fella. Good looking, too."

"What do you want?" the Queen says.

"I want you to meet my friend." The Cheshire welcomes Carolus inside.

"What is he doing here? We made a deal. I thought he was going to kill Alice while I ruled the world."

"Funny how none of this happened." The Cheshire enjoys a slump into a sofa and stretches his leg, his boot in the Queens face.

"You look like you want your head cut off," she said.

"You know you've never succeeded in doing that, not even in Wonderland."

"What do you want?" Margaret said.

"I want the four of us to be friends."

"And why would we accept that?" Margaret said.

"Because it seems to me like this Alice is *really* the Alice."

"I'm not going to listen to this nonsense again." The Queen stood up.

"Think about it. She had Carroll's key. And if that isn't proof enough, how about that she just bought the Inklings bar and is looking for the Six Members?"

The Queen's face tightened. "Who told her about the Inklings?"

"Doesn't matter." The Cheshire stood, too. "What matters is that, even if this girl is delusional, she isn't stopping. She has a heart made of breathing fire."

"Suppose she is," Margaret said. "Where is all of this going?"

"We need to start to work together. Let's forget our pasts and grudges and unite to get the Six Keys, and then we can bite at each other all we want."

Margaret looked at the Queen for advice.

"Listen," the Cheshire said. "Carolus is a madman when he needs his pill. I have incredible powers. Margaret is a ruthless woman. And you, My Queen, there is no one as evil as you are."

The Queen felt pleasure. She liked the compliment.

"So be it," she said. "If the Inklings are gathering, then I may as well welcome you and Carolus into Black Chess. But as long as you do as I say."

"Thank you," the Cheshire said.

"And don't ever grin in my presence. God. You're a creep."

"As you wish," he said. "Did you ever know Tom Truckle, the Radcliffe Asylum's director is a Wonderlander, by the way?"

"Why do you say that?"

"I tried to posses him, but couldn't."

"Can't be. I'm sure I'd recognize most Wonderlanders." The Queen dismissed him.

"If you say so," the Cheshire played with Jack's deck of cards. "Why should I care?" he shook his shoulders. "So what's our next move?"

"The third key, of course," Margaret interfered. "We have the one with the Pillar, and we know Alice has one. I may have an idea were the third one is."

"Great, but not now," The Queen said. "I need to play with my dogs for a while. And you, Cheshire, get rid of Jack's body. Jack is dead. I don't want to see him walking around."

"But, My Queen." The Cheshire couldn't help but flash his grin at her. "I'm planning to do horrible things with his body."

"How horrible?"

"Horrible as in using him to learn everything about this Alice girl."

"Now that's brilliant."

"And it'll get even better once I find the Tweedles."

Chapter 108

The Inklings, Oxford

I am cleaning the floor when the Pillar enters the bar.

"No news of Jack, yet?"

"Nothing," I say. "Like you said, I think he will just show up on his own like he always does."

"Can't argue much with a boy who is a figment of his own imagination." The Pillar knocks his cane on the ground. "How about you, are you feeling all right?"

"For letting a monster go?" I stare right at him. "Yeah. I'm fabulous."

"Listen. I didn't know the plague was only going to last for three days. Besides, killing Carolus will always kill Lewis."

"Did you notice that all we do is compile Wonderland Monsters one after the other? It's like I'm useless."

"You're not useless. You're learning. If you think you'll become an overnight hero like in comic books, you're dearly mistaken."

"And what about you, Pillar?" I put the broom aside.

"What about me?"

"Did you become a ruthless killer overnight, or did you have good training?"

"You're starting to sound like Fabiola."

"Maybe I should learn from her."

The Pillar reverts to silence.

"Look, I'm never going to forgive you for fooling me and taking the key. And I'm not going to ask what's with you, Fabiola, the kids, and the Executioner. I respect that each one of us has his own past," I try to be as forward as possible. Frankly, the man is irritable in all the wrong ways. "But be warned. Once I don't need to learn from you anymore, we won't talk again."

"I understand." He flips his cane. "Don't worry. I might be gone sooner than you think."

"Good." I try not to say a word so I don't soften to him in any way. Then the stubbornness inside me takes over. "Now, you need to leave. The Inklings only welcomes those who can walk on the white tiles of chess."

"I hate chess." He wiggles his nose. "But I wasn't here for this. I just met with the March Hare. He told me there is a small aftereffect for the plague that has just ended."

"What kind of aftereffect?"

"Everyone in the world will unwillingly tell the truth again from five to six PM today."

"Everyone? Us included?"

"Yes. It doesn't matter whether we smoked the hookah or not. It's kind of contagious. Everyone who was out there in the world for the last three days must have caught it."

"So it didn't end?"

"Actually it's nothing harmful, according to the March."

"How so?"

"He says the aftereffect is a bit personal. Everyone will either confront themselves with a truth or someone dear to them."

"A benign truth?"

"If you want to call it that."

"Okay then." I turn back to cleaning. "You need to go now."

"If I had a smoke every time I hear this," The Pillar mumbles. Then he hesitates, as if he wants to tell me something. I see him in the mirror on the wall. Fiddling with his cane.

The silence seems to stretch for ages. But eventually he turns around and leaves.

"Pillar," my tongue betrays me.

"Yes?"

"You think it's a bad thing that the only way the world experienced peace was to lie?"

"Only if you think the opposite of truth is lying." He doesn't turn around, his hands on the handle of the glass door.

"What's that supposed to mean?"

"It means it's true we avoid the truth at all costs every day in our lives. But we don't really lie. We make up things. Like a beautiful novel where we fake all our needs for a good hero. By the end of the book, you know it's fiction, that it's not true, but you'd be mistaken if you think it's false either."

My mind is reeling with ideas and metaphors again. How does he do that?

"Listen." I stand up. "I may have been a bit harsh on you."

"No, you weren't. I'm terrible." He opens the door to leave. "But don't worry," he sounds as if he's going to break my heart like no one has ever done before.

And he does. The last words the Pillar says almost bring me to my knees.

"You will not see me again for another fourteen years." The Pillar says, closes the door behind him, and disappears forever.

Epilogue Part One

London. The Hour of Truth, between 5 PM

In the hour of truth, Margaret Kent stood in front of her mirror again. She couldn't get her eyes off her fake beauty. All those plastic surgeries and the money she spent did a good job in fooling the citizens everywhere. Her face had earned her a few good jumps in her career, a lot of money, and even admiration and respect.

But if it was so good, why couldn't Margaret forget her own ugliness whenever she looked into this mirror?

Unable to help it, Margaret brought a chair and smashed it into the mirror. She hit it until her arms tired and her makeup thinned. Then she fell to the floor crying.

This hour of truth was incredibly devastating to her.

A few miles away, the Queen of Hearts also stared into the mirror. However, she didn't worry about her looks. She had made peace with her looks years ago. It wasn't the looks.

The Queen piled up chair after chair so she could stand on top of them. All she ever wanted was to be taller. Even a little bit taller would have sufficed. Every head she chopped was in hope to make others shorter – and so she'd be taller. If not in physical measures, then in the eyes of those she ruled.

Sometime she told herself she didn't really mean to kill anyone.

But the question always remained. How high could she stand on the chairs in front of the mirror?

At the highest point, where she felt a tinge of satisfaction, all the chairs tumbled down again.

Picking herself off the ground, she ran to the door and yelled. "Off with their heads!"

The guards looked puzzled, not sure whose head she wanted to chop off this time.

"I'm sorry, My Queen," one brave guard offered. "Whose head would you like us to cut off?"

"Since you opened your mouth"—she pouted—"Then it's you. Off with your head!"

How she wished the hour of truth would soon end.

As for Carolus, he now lived in a small room in the Queen's garden, waiting for his pills to calm him down every few hours. The rest of the time he kept reading that scary book called Alice in Wonderland. Oh, how it gave him a headache. He understood nothing of it and ended up looking forward to finding a way to put an end to this Lewis Carroll someday.

The truth brought nothing but headaches to him, so he gave in to sleep.

In the streets of London, the Cheshire had locked Jack in a basement while he strolled out, jumping from body to another.

The Cheshire used those people's bodies to do horrible things. The least of which was using the body of a ninety-year-old woman and lighting a car on fire.

But whatever he did, something was missing. What? It was simple. The Cheshire longed to know who he really was. Sure, he was a cat many, many years ago. But cats don't have names—no really, people make them up and think that the cats care.

In the hour of truth, the Cheshire realized that he could be anyone he ever wanted, except one: himself.

Farther and farther, Tom Truckle still kept the secret of his identity, which wasn't *that* hard to figure out, but most people just didn't notice. And to make sure he wouldn't feel the need to tell anyone, he locked himself up in the VIP floor of the asylum, now that the Pillar was gone.

But if the hour made him realize anything, then it was his utter loneliness in this world. His children didn't love him, nor did his wife, and hardly did anyone else.

Tom ended up talking to his best friend in the world. The flamingo, which turned out to be a perfectly lovable animal.

In the few last minutes of the hour of truth, he told the flamingo who he really was. The flamingo's eyes widened, wondering how no one ever noticed.

Epilogue Part Two

Oxford. The Hour of Truth, between 5:30 PM

Alice, at the hour of truth was a bit off her rocker. She was about to kill the lights in the Inklings when she saw Lewis Carroll sitting on one of the tables.

"I'm not imagining you, am I?"

"No," he said, resting one leg on another, his hands gently set on his legs. "It's one of the privileges of the Inklings. Sometimes I can pass through and meet you in this world."

"So what are you? Dead?" Alice stood frozen.

"It's complicated, and I don't have much time to tell," he said. "I'm here to thank you."

"Thank you!" His funny, curious rabbit peeked out of his pocket. "For what?"

"For not killing me—Carolus, I mean."

"Yeah, about that," Alice said. "How did you let that happen, Lewis? I can't believe something so evil could come out of you."

"It's a long story. Now is not the time to talk about it."

"Then what do you want to talk about?"

"That you have to stop worrying if you're the real Alice or not," he said. "I'm telling you, it's you."

"Yes, sure," she said reluctantly. "But how can I be sure you're real in the first place? How can I be sure anything is real?"

"How can anyone be sure, Alice? People walk in a haze all day. You think they're sure of anything? The trick isn't to be sure.

"Then what is the trick?"

"The trick to believe."

"Believe things are true no matter what?"

"No. Believe in yourself." He stood up. "I really need to go now, so again, thank you."

"You're welcome."

"By the way," he stopped before disappearing. "You never asked me why I was grateful you didn't kill Carolus."

"Isn't obvious? So you don't die?"

"Everyone dies, Alice," Lewis said. "I thanked you because if you have killed Carolus, I'd never have known if I could beat him myself"

Alice considered it for a moment. It was a good point of view. "Wait. I just realized you're showing up in the hour of truth. Does that mean you're real?"

But then Lewis was gone and the lights went out.

Epilogue Part Three

The Hour of Truth, between 5:43 PM.

In the Vatican, Fabiola sat alone in her private room in the back.

She was about to take off her white dress and fold it next to the Vorpal sword on the table.

Slowly, she began unbuttoning her dress. From this day, she was not going to be a nun anymore. It had only been a matter of time.

She stared at her arms and shoulders, and almost closed her eyes. They showed traces of her past in the most unusual ways.

Fabiola changed into a modern dress, jeans and a t-shirt, took her Vorpal sword and opened the door.

She stopped by the children from Columbia. The children nodded understandably. They knew what was going on, and they liked it.

Then Fabiola walked past the people who loved her and cherished her.

Smiling at her followers, she cursed the Pillar under her breath. She cursed him for so many things, but mainly for reminding her she was no nun. That no matter how she tried to hide it, she was a warrior. And World War Wonderland was only a week or two away.

Some of her people cupped their hands on their mouth, staring at her arms. Was this the nun they had loved and cherished all along?

But Fabiola had no choice. Black Chess surfaced. The Inklings were gathering. The prophecy had proven to be right. The girl was the Real Alice, even if she didn't always seem apt to the mission.

She stepped out of the church, asking to be forgiven, for she was about to stare darkness in the eyes, hoping she'd be as strong as Alice and not get stained like in the past.

She turned and said goodbye to her people, still staring at her hands and shoulders covered in tattoos. She knew it was shocking, even to herself after all this time. But she could not escape who she really was. The Pillar made sure she'd return to her old self, and she hated him for that.

Throughout the piazza, walked the White Queen, gripping her Vorpal sword, wearing the tattoos that mostly said:

I can't escape yesterday because I'm still the same warrior now.

On the other side of the world, the Pillar was sitting on a bank in Oxford University when the hour of truth came. He'd managed to resist the truth for half an hour. But it was no use. Whatever this curse of truth was, it was madder than fiction.

He was fiddling with the key when the hour's effect empowered him. There was no going back now.

He pulled out an envelope and tucked the key in.

Slowly, he walked out of the university to the nearest post office. He borrowed a pen and wrote on a small piece of paper:

Here is the first key. Alice has another, so you have two out of six now. As for me, mission accomplished. I'm done and gone. None of you will ever see me again.

The Pillar slid the piece of paper into the envelope and licked it to a close.

He borrowed the pen again and wrote on the back of the envelope:

To the only woman I've ever loved.

Then he wrote the address on the back: The Vatican.

While trying to slide the envelope into the box, his glove stuck in a nail sticking out from the side. He took off the white glove, just for a moment, and found himself staring at an old heart-wrenching memory. He was staring at the two knuckles missing from the fingers on his right hand.

The END...
Alice will return in Insanity 5

Thank You

Thank you for purchasing this insane book. I'm so happy, and grateful, to be able to share this story with you, and I hope you enjoyed reading it as much as I enjoyed lying to you!

Hookah is a special episode in the series to me. It's a stepping stone, where I realized the series isn't just about Alice and the Pillar. I realized how every character was slowly coming alive, villain or hero, whether I liked it or not. How Lewis Carroll created such rich individuals is beyond me, but I'm chugging my way into who they could really have been.

A few facts about Hookah:

Phantasmagoria is a real mysterious poem from Lewis Carroll. No one's sure, as far as I know, if it's related to the art of Phantasmagoria – which you can *google* and learn more about if you're interested. The Dodo in the Nasca Lines had always been a mystery, and whether it had anything to do with Lewis, especially that it's an extinct bird now, I'm not sure. And Mr. Nobody is a real character in Carroll's book. He's always fascinated me. All jokes, the good the bad and the lame, are Carroll's jokes, some of them you can find in The Hunting of the Snark and his diaries. The Inklings is real, and the facts about it are true.

As for Lewis Carroll's migraines, there are no doubts about him suffering some kind of recurrent headache and pain. It's documented in his diaries. There is even a missing drawing where he'd drawn his head missing half of it – split personality? Of course, Carolus Ludovicus isn't real, but the name Lewis Carroll chose in Latin to create his Pen name. I created him to show the painful side of artists in general. In this case, I used Lewis Carroll as a vehicle. All respect and love to the people of Columbia, Peru, and Brazil; none of the storylines were meant to be anything but entertainment and mad fiction.

Lastly, I know the Pillar and Fabiola's story is now more of a mystery, and I already got this question from my lovely beta readers: is the Pillar gone for good?

The answer is: I can't say.

Also, I don't have a name for Insanity 5 yet, but stay tuned. It won't be long before it's released.

I'd like to remind you to follow the special Pinterest page, where you can see for yourself all the places and riddles Alice and Pillar visited—I always update it when I get my hands on new pictures, as long as they don't spoil the main plot. You can access it by visiting pinterest.com/camjace

Please stay tuned to my Facebook Page: Facebook.com/camjace or cameronjace.com for more information.

If you have a question, please message me on Facebook; I love connecting with all of my readers, because without you, none of this would be possible.

Thank you, for everything.
Cameron.

Subscribe to Cameron's Mailing List

To receive exclusive updates from Cameron Jace and to be the first to get your hands on Insanity 5, please sign up to be on his personal mailing list!

You'll get instant access to cover releases and chapter previews, and you'll be the only readers to be eligible to win prices!

cameronjace.com

About the Author

Cameron Jace is the boy next door who managed, by some miracle, to become the bestselling author of the Grimm Diaries series and the Insanity series. A graduate of the College of Architecture, and a devout collector of out-of-print books, he is obsessed with the origins of folk tales and the mysterious storytellers who first told them. Three of his books made Amazon's Top 100 Customer Favorites in Kindle 2013 and Amazon's Top 100 kindle list. Cameron lives in California with his girlfriend. When he isn't writing or collecting books, he is reading or playing his guitar.